www.melvinbeederman.com

# MELVIN BEEDERMAN
# SUPERHERO

## THE BROTHERHOOD
## OF THE
## TRAVELING UNDERPANTS

### GREG TRINE

ILLUSTRATED BY
## RHODE MONTIJO

SQUARE
FISH

HENRY HOLT AND COMPANY ★ NEW YORK

*For Juanita*
—G. T.

*For my brother Michael*
—R. M.

SQUARE
FISH

An Imprint of Macmillan

THE BROTHERHOOD OF THE TRAVELING UNDERPANTS.
Text copyright © 2009 by Greg Trine.
Illustrations copyright © 2009 by Rhode Montijo.
All rights reserved. Printed in the United States of America by
R. R. Donnelley & Sons Company, Harrisonburg, Virginia. For information, address
Square Fish, 175 Fifth Avenue, New York, NY 10010.

Square Fish and the Square Fish logo are trademarks of Macmillan and
are used by Henry Holt and Company under license from Macmillan.

Library of Congress Cataloging-in-Publication Data
Trine, Greg.
The Brotherhood of the Traveling Underpants / Greg Trine ;
art by Rhode Montijo.
p.    cm.    – (Melvin Beederman, superhero ; bk. 7)
Summary: When the three members of the Bad Guy Brotherhood buy a time machine
to keep the younger Melvin from gaining his superhero powers, Melvin and his
sidekick Candace, disguised as pirates, travel back in time to stop them.
ISBN 978-0-8050-8163-3
[1. Superheroes–Fiction. 2. Time travel–Fiction. 3. Los Angeles (Calif.)–Fiction.
4. Humorous stories.] I. Montijo, Rhode, ill. II. Title.
PZ7.T7356Br 2009        [Fic]–dc22        2008037306

Originally published in the United States by Henry Holt and Company
First Square Fish Edition: October 2012
Square Fish logo designed by Filomena Tuosto
Hand-lettering by David Gatti
mackids.com

7   9   10   8

AR: 3.8 / LEXILE: 560L

# CONTENTS

# THE BAD GUY BROTHERHOOD

Goofball McCluskey was the brains of the operation. Calamity Wayne had the getaway vehicle. And Max the Wonder Thug was, of course, the muscle. If you wanted something broken, you called Max. If you wanted to get away after breaking something, you called Calamity. And if you wanted to know *how* to do both perfectly, you asked Goofball.

Speaking of Goofball . . .

"We have to do it before school lets out," Goofball said. He was sitting at the table with Calamity and Max discussing plans for their latest job—a bank robbery. With the McNasty Brothers in prison, the bank-robbing business was wide open. "If we pull the job after school, we'll have two superheroes to deal with instead of one."

Max nodded. "Good thinking," he said, scratching his oversized neck.

The three bad guys met weekly for the Bad Guy Brotherhood, where they discussed various bad guy ideas and got feedback from one another. They used to call their meetings the Sinister Sessions. Before that they called themselves the Brotherhood of the Traveling Underpants, but being connected by a shared article of clothing seemed a bit odd—and kind of gross.

Calamity looked confused. "Two superheroes instead of one?"

"That's right," Goofball said. "Melvin

Beederman has a sidekick. He only works alone until his sidekick gets out of school. Everyone knows that. I'd rather deal with one superhero instead of two, wouldn't you?"

"Of course," Calamity said. Calamity could be a bit slow sometimes, but he eventually understood. If they pulled the job in the morning, then Melvin would be working alone, which would make it easier to get away.

These bad guys weren't stupid. Okay, maybe one of them was. But two out of three ain't bad.*

---

* The narrator usually doesn't use the word *ain't*, but he decided to break the rules in this case, because sometimes there just ain't a better way to say something. Oops, he did it again!

Melvin Beederman
was the superhero in
charge of Los Angeles. He
lived alone in a tree house overlooking
the city. Candace Brinkwater was his
sidekick, his partner in uncrime, the girl
he had divided his cape with. She was
the only person ever to score 500 points
in a single game of
basketball. She was
the only one ever to run
the hundred-yard dash
in three and a half sec-
onds. She was the only
third-grader who
could fly.

But she had to wait until after school to help Melvin save the world. And so Goofball, Max, and Calamity planned their devious and sinister deeds for when Candace wasn't around to help her partner in uncrime.

The three bad guys raised their glasses in a toast to their evil plan. Max, the muscle, would beat up the security guard at the bank, Goofball would get the money, and Calamity would drive the getaway vehicle.

"Be sure to make like a baker and haul buns!" Max told Calamity.

"Exactly!" Goofball said.

"No problem," Calamity said.

With any luck, they'd get the job done. If only they could outsmart Melvin Beederman. After all, Melvin had graduated from the Superhero Academy. And he had noggin power!

## BREAKFAST OF CHAMPIONS

Our superhero was in a pickle. Really! It was a pickle with a V-8 engine and a five-speed transmission. Zero to sixty in 59 seconds. Okay, maybe it wasn't a very fast pickle, which is why the bad guys were getting away.

And laughing while they did.

Our superhero put his head out the window and yelled for his sidekick.

Suddenly the ground shook.

Windows rattled. And there she was, running alongside the pickle. "You rang, boss?" she said.

"No, Thunder Thighs. I yelled. Now help me catch these bad guys."

She did. Thunderman and his assistant Thunder Thighs caught the bad guys, just in time for commercials.

Melvin Beederman had been watching *The Adventures of Thunderman* with his pet rat Hugo while eating his normal breakfast of pretzels and root beer. Now he turned off the TV and stretched.

"Luckily he had Thunder Thighs to help," Melvin said to Hugo. "Thunderman needs to get a new pickle, don't you think?"

"Squeak," said the rat.

This either meant "I'd recommend a Harley-Davidson" or "Are you going to eat that last pretzel?" Melvin was never sure what Hugo was saying. Back at the Superhero Academy he had been fluent in gerbil, but rat language was not the same thing. For example, they said "warthog" differently, and that was only the beginning.

It was a fine day for saving the world, Melvin thought as he looked out over the city of Los Angeles. The sun was

shining, the birds were singing, even Hugo was humming as he started playing his mini guitar.

Melvin tied his cape around his neck and looked at himself in the—

*Sirens!* He could hear them blaring with his extra-sensitive hearing. Trouble was brewing! He could feel it.

Melvin launched himself. "Up, up, and away!"

*Crash!* He hit the ground.

He got up and tried again. "Up, up, and away!"

*Splat!*

"Up, up, and away!"

*Thud!*

*Kabonk!*

On the fifth try he was up and flying.

This was how it went for Melvin Beederman. He never got off the ground on the first try. But no matter. He was up and flying, streaking toward downtown. Bad guys, beware! Melvin Beederman was on the job. And he wasn't driving a pickle.

# TROUBLE ON LAIR HILL

Goofball, the brains of the operation, chose a bank in Beverly Hills for the robbery. The city was full of rich people, and that meant their banks were full of loot. Not money—loot. This was bad guy lingo, of course. Normal people called it money. Criminals called it loot.

Max the Wonder Thug knocked out the bank security guard with one punch. Goofball McCluskey jumped behind the counter and grabbed all the loot he could get his hands on. Outside, Calamity Wayne waited in the getaway vehicle—it wasn't a pickle. He could hear the sirens getting louder.

And louder.

Little did he know that Melvin Beederman was already on the job.

"Hurry up, you guys!" Calamity yelled out the window. "Let's hit the road." He had nothing against roads and he wasn't really sure why he wanted to hit one. He just knew that he wanted to get out of there ASAP—maybe sooner.

"Let's go!" Calamity yelled again as the sirens grew louder. "Hurry!"

A few seconds later the front doors of the bank flew open. Goofball and Max,

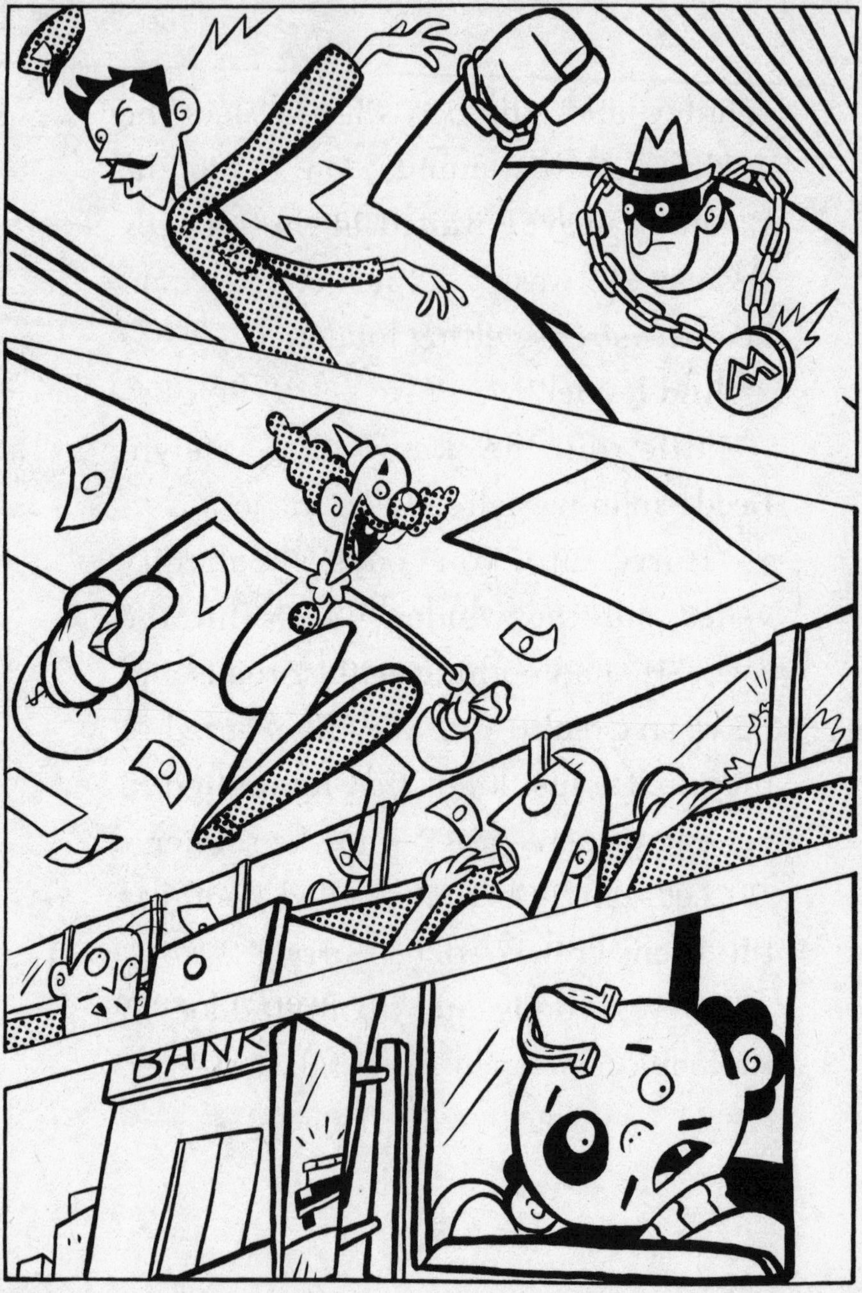
BANK

loaded down with money . . . uh, loot . . . ran for the car.

"Let's make like a banana and split," Max said.

Calamity looked confused again, although he loved bananas. "What does that mean?"

"Hit the road . . . now!"

"What did the road ever do to you?" Calamity had been feeling guilty about the whole hitting-the-road business.

"Back to our evil lair!" Goofball yelled. "Can't you hear those sirens?"

Calamity did hear them. He stepped on the gas and turned off onto a side street, just in time. Just in the nick of time, to be exact. They weren't seen by the police. But that didn't mean they weren't seen by a certain superhero.

Melvin Beederman flew over the city. It may have taken him many attempts to get up and flying, but once he was airborne, he was as good as they come. He zigged, he zagged, he swooped. He paused briefly in front of a building to flex and admire his reflection in the glass. And that's when he saw a suspicious-looking vehicle heading for Lair Hill, which is where lots of bad guys lived. Movie stars moved to the Hollywood Hills; bad guys moved to Lair Hill.

With his x-ray vision, Melvin could see through the metal roof of the car. He could also see the underwear of the three occupants. Disgusting! Bad guys never wore clean underwear. Even some good guys didn't. Melvin tried to ignore it. He was on the job. He was looking for—

Hey! Wasn't that money in the car? Bags of it? These were the bank robbers, all right. Melvin followed them to Lair Hill. He wanted to find out where their lair was in case there were more evil bad guys to catch. Besides, he wanted to kick in the front door, which, of course, was one of the perks of being a superhero. He loved kicking in doors.

The car pulled up in front of a two-story building. It was an average lair as lairs go. Melvin waited until they had dragged the bags of money inside and

closed the door. Then he swooped down
out of the sky and kicked it in.

"Not so fast!" he yelled. This
was part of the Superhero's

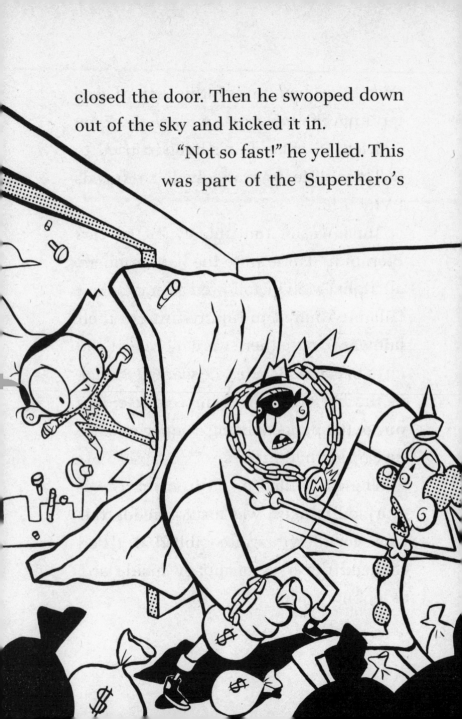

Code. You had to say this before you captured the bad guys.

"Get him, Max," Goofball said.

This time Max looked confused. "Why me?"

"Because I am the brains of the operation," Goofball said.

"I just drive the getaway vehicle," Calamity Wayne added, running for the side door.

"Not so fast!" Melvin said again. "It means the jig is up." He wasn't really sure what a jig was or why the heck it was up, but it sure sounded good, and it felt great to say.

Max attacked. Goofball ran for the back door. But Melvin grabbed all three of them before you could say, "I'm tired of looking at dirty underwear." He was.

He hauled them outside and lifted off the ground. At least he tried to.

"Up, up, and away!"

*Crash!* "Ouch!" said the three bad guys.

*Splat!* "Ouch!"

*Thud!* "Ouch!"

*Kabonk!* "Ouch!"

It was bad enough being captured by a superhero, but being captured by one with flying problems was kind of embarrassing. Plus, it really hurt!

On the fifth try, Melvin was up and flying. He carried Goofball, Max, and Calamity to jail, where they belonged.

"Curses!" Goofball said.

"You can say that again," Calamity said.

"Curses!"

Max didn't say anything. But he really wanted to make like some blackberries and jam. Or possibly make like a nose and run.

# THE NOT-SO-GREAT ESCAPE

The prison where they sent Goofball, Max, and Wayne was very crowded, so much so that the warden put all three of them in the same cell until he could find room for them. Unfortunately, this was the very cell they had used to hold Grunge McNasty, that notorious bank robber and all-around bad guy. On the floor of the cell was a large piece of plywood and beneath it was a hole in the floor, leading to the tunnel dug by the McNasty Sisters when they broke their brothers out of prison.

"Holy dumb prison workers!" said Goofball. "Let's get out of here."

Holy dumb prison workers, indeed! They did. They jumped into the hole and followed the tunnel to freedom. Once outside the prison, they ran. They ran and ran and ran. But where to go? They couldn't go back to their lair on Lair Hill. The police already knew about it. More important, so did Melvin Beederman.

Speaking of Melvin . . .

"We have to do something about Melvin Beederman," Goofball said, "or we'll never be able to pull any more sinister or devious deeds. Any ideas?"

Max was busy doing push-ups. He stopped and thought. He couldn't flex his muscles and think at the same time.

Calamity put on his thinking cap. It was green with white stripes.

"We need a new place to live, and we need to find a way to get rid of Melvin Beederman," said Goofball. He looked at his two companions. Calamity wasn't known for his ability to think, but that didn't mean Max didn't have any ideas.

"How about Big Al's?" Max said.

"Yes, Big Al will know what to do," Goofball said.

Big Al's Rent-a-Lair was the place to go if you were a bad guy looking for a place to live. He also sold all kinds of bad guy gadgets, things to make a good guy's life miserable. If anyone could help them with their Beederman problems, Big Al could. After all, Big Al had been serving Southern California's bad guys since 1985.

"Can I interest you in a new lair?" Al asked, when Goofball and Company arrived.

"Yes," Goofball said. "We'd also like to see what you have in the defeat-a-superhero department."

Big Al nodded. He knew which super-hero they had in mind. "I think I may have just the thing. It's in my office. Follow me." The three bad guys followed Al past the latest lair models in the showroom to the office in the back of the store. He pointed to a large box.

"What is it?" Max asked.

"It's the very latest thing. You want to get rid of Melvin Beederman, right? This is the way to do it."

Of course, this didn't exactly answer Max's question. "What is it?" he asked again.

"It's a time machine," Big Al said proudly. "Melvin Beederman is one tough superhero. He's faster than you. He's stronger than you. He can see your underwear."

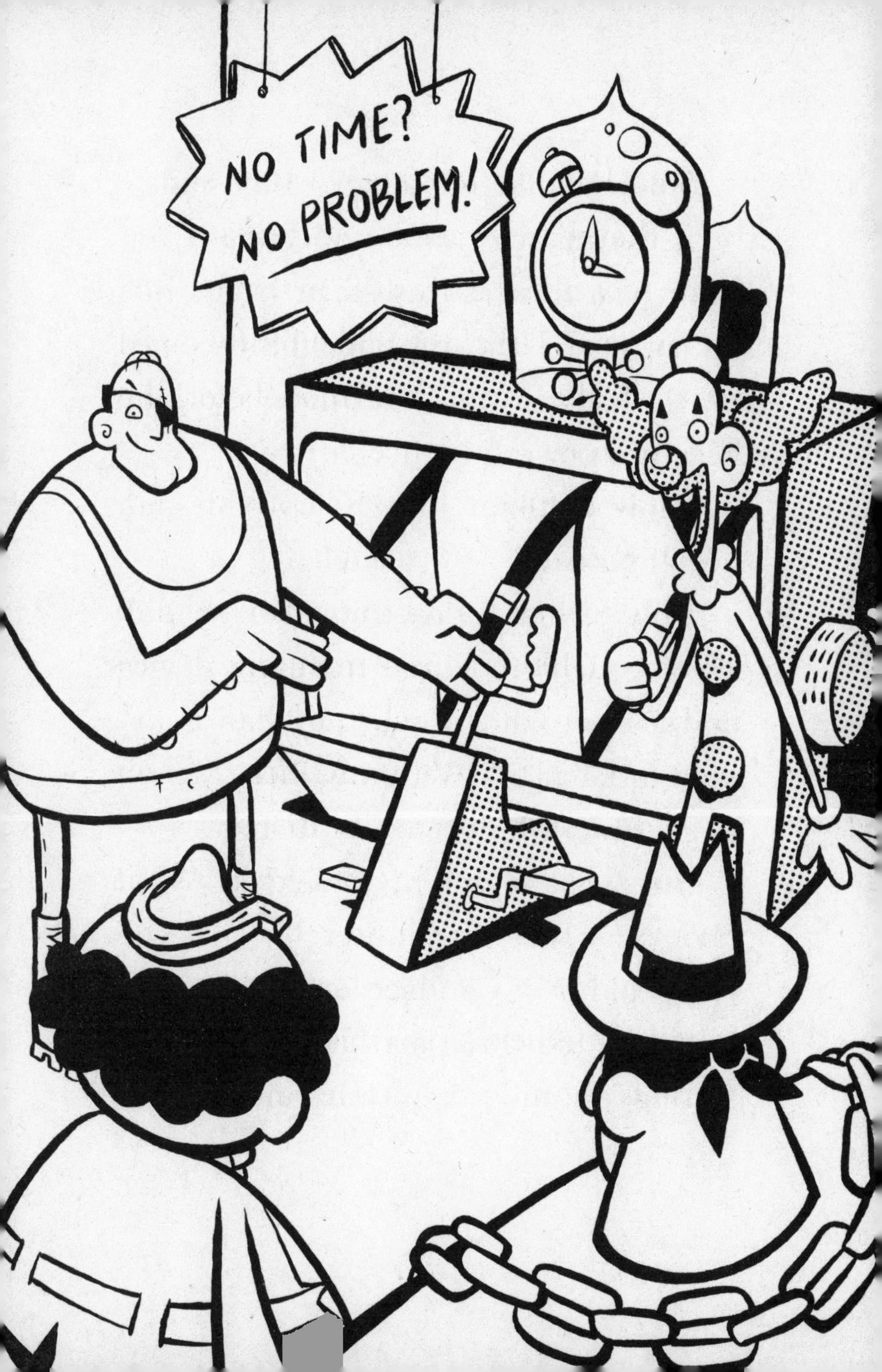
NO TIME?
NO PROBLEM!

"You can say that again," Max said.

"He can see your underwear. You can't beat him at this stage in his life. That's where the time machine comes in. Go back in time. Get him before he becomes powerful."

"Holy brilliant idea!" Goofball said. "We'll take it."

Holy brilliant idea, indeed! They did. They bought the time traveling device and a basic lair, which they had delivered to Lair Hill. With any luck, Melvin Beederman would soon be history.

But what about his sidekick? What about Candace Brinkwater?

Speaking of Candace Brinkwater . . .

While the three bad guys were busy setting up their new lair and putting together their time machine, Melvin Beederman was with his partner in uncrime, Candace Brinkwater. School had just let out, and the two of them met at the public library so that Melvin could help her with math. This was how it went every day. Melvin helped Candace with math, and she helped him save the world.

"What's the latest?" Candace asked as she worked an addition problem.

"Bad news. Goofball McCluskey, Max the Wonder Thug, and Calamity Wayne escaped from prison."

"Holy I'm-one-peeved-sidekick!"

Holy she's-one-peeved-sidekick, indeed! She was. She hated when the bad guys escaped from prison. But at

least it gave her something to do . . .
after her homework was finished, that is.

"You forgot to carry the one," Melvin
said, pointing to Candace's worksheet.
"Hurry up. We have to catch those guys."

# MEANWHILE...

While Candace was finishing her math, Goofball, Max, and Calamity were hard at work putting together their time machine. It was a battery-operated model, and it had three seats. It would be perfect, Goofball decided. They'd all travel back in time together.

"Is this thing powered by the flux capacitor?" Max asked. He thought he had seen something like that in an old movie.

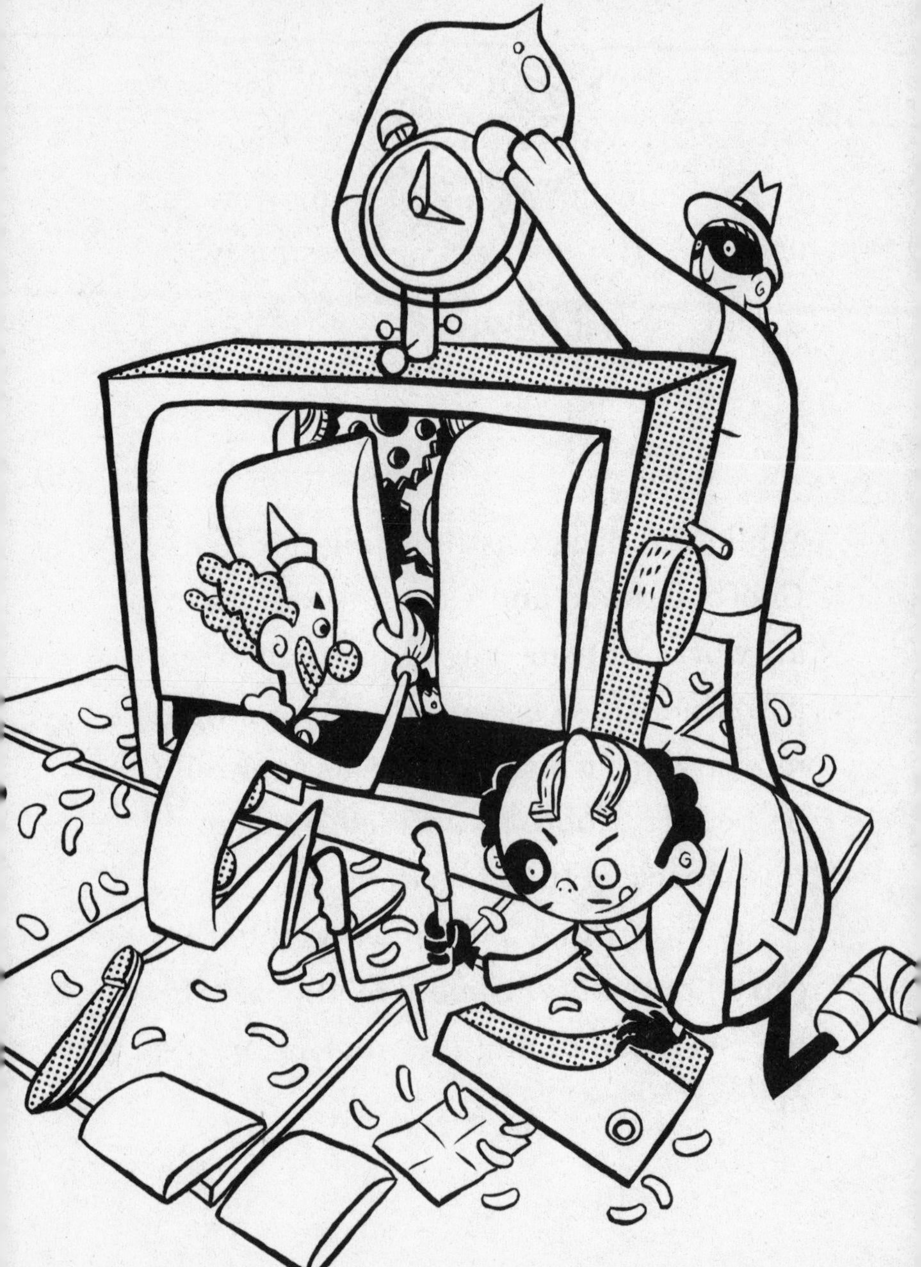

"No. This is powered by the slip transistor or the slide battery." Goofball didn't know how the darn thing worked, actually. He just liked messing with Max, which was one of his hobbies.

"How should I know?" Goofball said finally. "Hand me that wrench." He fastened the final bolt and stood back to admire their new mode of travel. It looked sinister all right—sinister with a capital S. Or devious. Take your pick.

"Ain't she a beauty?" Max ran his hand along the pinstriping. "I bet this baby goes from zero to sixty in way less than 59 seconds."

"Yes, if this thing's as slow as Thunderman's pickle, I'm going to shoot myself." Goofball circled the device a few times, looking for any flaws. He had to admit, it really was a beauty. The question was: Would it work? Would it transport them back so that they could get Melvin Beederman before he became powerful?

Goofball stopped and looked at his partners in crime. "Where was Melvin Beederman before he came to Los Angeles?"

"The Superhero Academy," Calamity said. Calamity wasn't the brightest bulb in the chandelier, but even he knew that. "Los Angeles is Melvin's first job since graduating."

"Then that's where we're headed, boys." Goofball began making notes. "When was he at the academy? Can you give me the exact dates?"

Max and Calamity gave the information to Goofball, who wrote it down. "This is perfect. Melvin Beederman won't suspect a thing," he said with an evil laugh.

As evil laughs go, Goofball had a great one. He had been the National Evil Laugh Champion three years in a row, and that ain't bad.

That ain't bad, indeed! Oops!

"Who said that?" Max asked.

"Who said what?"

"Who said 'oops'?"

"The narrator."

Max scratched his oversized neck. "That's strange. Why didn't he just put the 'oops' as a footnote on the bottom of the page?"

It was horrible being in a story where the narrator was obviously off his rocker.

# HOLY
# WHAT-THE-HECK-WAS-THAT?

Off his rocker, indeed! But let's get back to our story.

Yes, Goofball and Company had their time machine ready to go, but all was not well on Lair Hill. Melvin Beederman and Candace Brinkwater were on patrol, and they were closing in.

"What do you see, Melvin?" Candace asked as they scanned the lairs below.

"Dirty underwear, and way too much of it!"

"Besides that."

Melvin held up a hand. "Hold on. I hear something." He hovered in place and listened. It was coming from one of the lairs. "Some guys are discussing the narrator."

"So?" Candace said.

"So it may be Goofball and Company. Come on." Melvin zoomed ahead and Candace followed.

Discussing the narrator wasn't a sure sign that it was the bad guys they were looking for. Maybe it was a book club. But something, or someone, told Melvin that he was on the right track. Actually, what told him was the guy telling the story.

But that's a little too much narrator intrusion, even for *this* book.

Melvin dropped a little lower and continued to listen. "Now they're talking about something else. Time travel."

"I hear it," Candace said, gazing at her partner in uncrime. "They're saying something about Melvin Beederman, too."

Goofball McCluskey set the dials on the time machine for when Melvin was still at the academy. This was going to be fun, he thought. "Strap in, guys," he told Max and Calamity. "Let's go make his life miserable."

The three partners in crime took their places in the time machine and fastened their seat belts. The directions said that re-entry could be a little rough. You had to be strapped in to avoid injury.

"Ready?" Goofball asked.

"Roger that," Max said.

"Who's Roger?" Calamity asked.

Goofball pushed the START button and the machine roared to life. "Hold on! Here we go."

They did. But not right away. Not before the machine got louder and louder. Loud enough to attract the attention of a couple of superheroes.

Melvin and Candace swooped from the sky. They found the house where the guys had been discussing the narrator. It was the same place where they had been discussing time travel—and Melvin Beederman. Now there was some machine making all kinds of noise.

Melvin pointed to the front door of the lair. "Candace, do the honors." It was her turn to kick in the door. He'd kicked in the last one.

"GLADLY," Candace shouted above the sound of the screaming machine.

She kicked in the door. Then she and Melvin rushed into the room.

"Not so fast!" Melvin said. But they were too late. They caught a glimpse of three men seat-belted into some kind of machine. And then it vanished right before their eyes.

"Holy what-the-heck-was-that?" Melvin said.

Holy what-the-heck-was-that, indeed! Don't you know a time machine when you see it, Melvin? He didn't.

Melvin looked at his partner in uncrime. "Was I seeing things, or did three guys just disappear?"

"I saw it, too," Candace said. "And not just any guys . . . that was Goofball McCluskey, Max the Wonder Thug, and Calamity Wayne."

"Yes." Melvin nodded. "I'd recognize Max's thick neck anywhere."

The two superheroes began looking around the room for clues. It didn't take

a genius to realize something sinister was afoot. Or maybe it was something devious. And maybe it wasn't a foot—it could have been an ankle. The point is, you have to be concerned when three of the worst criminals in Los Angeles vanish before your eyes.

Candace walked over to a table that was covered with sheets of paper. "Melvin, look at this."

"Looks like directions for putting together a time machine," Melvin said. He picked up a sheet for a closer look. When he did he saw a note beneath it: *Melvin Beederman . . . Superhero Academy.*

"Any ideas, Candace?"

"Hmm. Your name, the name of your school, and a time machine," Candace said, staring at the papers on the table. "Why would bad guys want to travel in time?"

"They're history buffs?" suggested Melvin. He shook his head. No, it was something else.

"Do you think they went into the future?" Candace asked.

Melvin thought about this. Then looked again at the paper with his name and school. "Holy my-goose-is-cooked! No, not the future. The *past!*" Melvin pointed. "They are headed to the Superhero Academy to get me—the younger me!"

Holy his-goose-is-cooked, indeed! That was a fine bit of detective thinking, Melvin. But how are you going to go back in time without a time machine?

"How am I, indeed!" Melvin said.

Candace looked confused. It wasn't easy being in a story when you didn't know who was narrating.

## SUPERHERO PIRATES

It took some more detective work for the two partners in uncrime to figure out where the time machine had come from. But not much, because the sales receipt was right there among the papers on the table, and it had all the information they needed.

"I should have known," Melvin said. He turned to his assistant. "Looks like Big Al is now selling time machines."

Candace made a face like she had bitten into a Brussels sprout and worm sandwich. "It was much easier when he was just selling lairs. What'll we do, wait until midnight and break in?"

"There's no time for that. Goofball, Max, and Calamity are already headed for the academy. We have to go to Big Al's now."

"He knows what we look like," Candace said. "And you know he never sells things to good guys."

Melvin nodded. It was true. Al's usual customers were bad guys. He might not want to give the superheroes any information at all, let alone sell them a time machine. If word got out that he was helping crime fighters, his business would go down the drain—followed by Al himself.

"Let's go," Melvin said. They ran outside. "Up, up, and away!"

*Crash!*

He tried again.

*Splat!*

Some things never change.

*Thud!*

*Kabonk!*

On the fifth try Melvin was up and flying. He joined Candace, who was waiting for him above the trees and filing her nails. She always brought something to keep herself busy while Melvin tried to launch himself.

Candace put her file away and turned to Melvin. "What's the plan?"

"We'd better disguise ourselves," he said. "What have you got in your closet?"

"You'd make an excellent pirate," Candace said.

"Holy swashbuckler!" Melvin said.

Holy swashbuckler, indeed! Melvin had never been a pirate before. He'd once dressed up as Peter Pan for Halloween, but that's as close as he'd gotten.

Melvin and Candace flew to her

house and went upstairs to her bed-room. Candace began pulling things out of her closet. "Which do you prefer, a peg leg or an eye patch?"

Melvin thought this over. He'd rather limp than not be able to see. "Peg leg," he said.

"Peg leg, it is."

They dressed quickly. Soon they were looking very pirate-ish.

"How are your acting skills, Candace?" Melvin asked as he looked at himself in the closet mirror. His peg leg looked fabulous.

"Acting? Heck, it's what I used to do before I started saving the world. You should have seen me play Little Red Riding Hood."

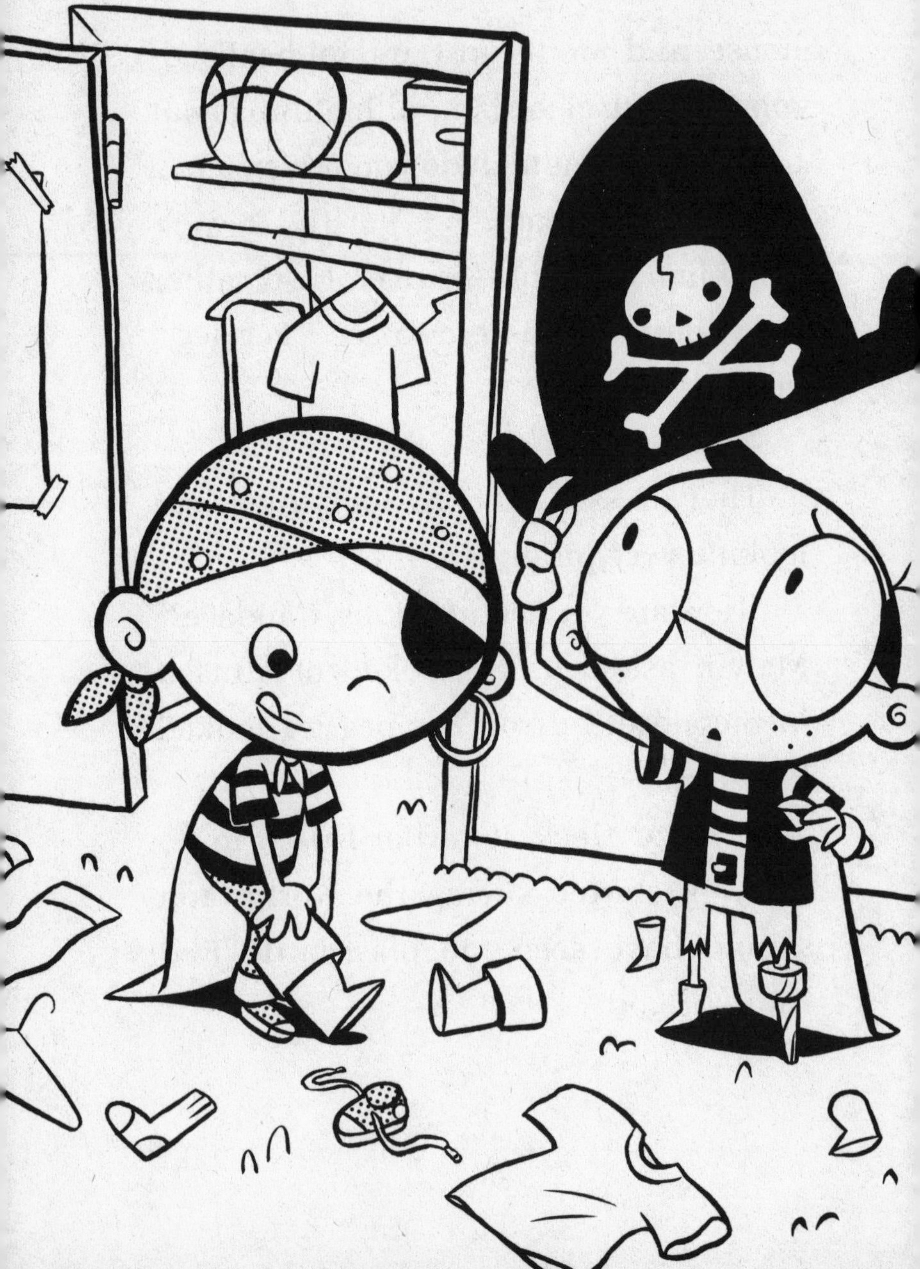

"Great. Then I'll let you do the talking when we get to Al's."

"Aye, aye, matey. Let's go."

They did. But they didn't fly. Pirates streaking across the sky might look a little suspicious. In fact, pirates with capes were a little weird.

## CLANKITY–WHUMP–POW–THUNK!

Meanwhile Goofball, Max, and Calamity were traveling back in time. Then they came to a sudden stop with a *clankity–whump–pow–thunk!* Just as the directions warned, re-entry was a little rough. But the sound effects were very cool.

"Very cool, indeed!" Goofball said, untangling himself from his partners in crime. He had always loved good sound effects.

"Who do you think you are? The narrator?" Max asked.

"Sorry."

The three of them looked around. They were standing on Lair Hill, but their lair was nowhere to be seen. This made sense. They'd gone back in time, but they hadn't changed locations. Their lair wasn't there because they hadn't bought it yet.

The problem was, of course, they were still in Los Angeles, and the Superhero Academy was in Boston. They'd still have to travel across the country to get to the younger, less-powerful Melvin Beederman. There was only one way to get there, Goofball decided. Fly!

"Calamity Wayne, can you fly a plane?"

"Are you kidding?" Max said. "He'd love to make like an insect and fly."

This was true. He really would. It was what he lived for. Calamity Wayne could operate any kind of contraption that carried passengers. Planes, trains, automobiles—you name it, he could make it go.

"We need a plane," Goofball said.

"And we need one now . . . sooner if possible!"

While Goofball and Company were looking for a plane to steal, Melvin and Candace had arrived at Big Al's Rent-a-Lair. Big Al himself was busy showing off the latest lairs in his showroom. The store was currently having a half-off sale, and any bad guy with half a brain would act now—including ones who looked like pirates.

"Take this baby, for example," Al said, slapping the side of a lair. "You won't find a better—"

"What do you have in a time machine?" Candace said. She adjusted her eye patch and put on her serious bad guy look.

*She's good,* Melvin thought, limping around on his peg leg. He loved the sound it made . . . *click thud click thud.* He had always appreciated good sound effects, too.

She *was* good. Good enough to fool Al anyway.

"Time machine, you say?" Al cracked his knuckles and smiled. This was good news. Time machines cost even more than lairs. He'd make a bundle off these two . . . pirates? He'd never seen pirates with capes before. But anyone with money to spend was okay by him. He was an equal opportunity greedy person.

"Would you like it gift wrapped?" Al asked. "We also offer free delivery."

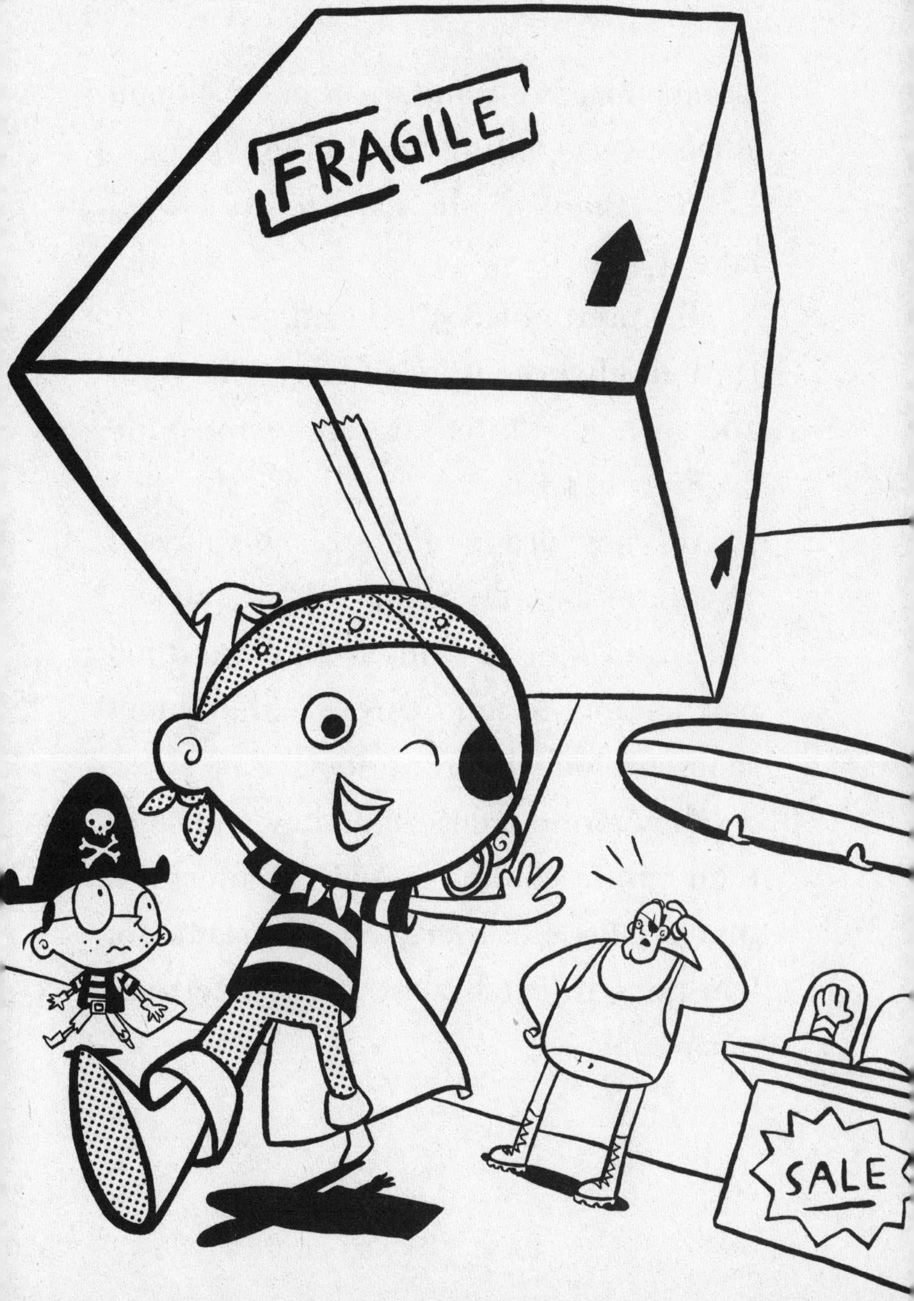
FRAGILE
SALE

Melvin gave Candace a hand signal, since he was letting her do the talking.

"No, thanks," she said to Al. "We'll take it as is."

"It's pretty heavy," Al said.

"I can handle it," Candace said. With one arm she lifted the time machine over her head.

Al's jaw dropped at this display of strength. "How on earth—?"

"Yoga," Melvin said, and followed his partner in uncrime through the showroom and out the front door.

They found a deserted alley and shed their pirate clothes. Melvin would miss that peg leg, but there were things to do, bad guys to catch, a young Beederman to save.

They assembled the time machine quickly, then Melvin pulled out a piece of paper he'd taken from the bad guy lair. On it was written the date when he was still at the academy. He set the dials on the time machine.

"Ready, Candace?"

She nodded, then Melvin pressed the START button.

## AAAAAAAHHHHHH!

"We could make like a golf club," Max suggested.

"What?" Goofball asked.

"We could make like a golf club and drive."

Goofball shook his head. "It'll take too long. Flying is the only way."

Calamity loved Max's idea of making like a golf club, but making like an insect was faster. He just happened to hate insects. Tiger Woods, on the other hand, was his hero.

They went to the local airport and looked around. "How about that one?" Calamity pointed to a small red plane with the words BUBBA'S EXPERT CROP DUSTING written on the side.

"Perfect!" Goofball said. He turned to Max. "Do what you do best, Max."

This meant, of course, that he should smack Bubba, the owner of the plane. Max did just that. One punch and Bubba was out cold.

"Let's make like a tree and—"

"No time to make like anything," Goofball said, running for the plane. "Let's go!"

The three of them jumped into the

plane, Calamity started it up, and then they took off into the wild blue. Yonder, that is.

*Clankity–Whump–Pow–Thunk!* While the bad guys were heading into the wild blue, Melvin and Candace were coming through a rough re-entry. They had forgotten to strap in, and it wasn't at all pretty. In fact, it was pretty ugly.

They'd gone back in time, just as Goofball and Company had. But they still had to get to Boston, the location of the academy and the younger Melvin.

"Let's go." Melvin got to his feet and launched himself.

This is what he tried to do at least. It took him five tries after the usual *Crash! Splat! Thud! Kabonk!* He joined Candace in the air, who was keeping herself busy juggling tangerines she'd plucked from a nearby tree.

"Boston, here we come," Melvin said. They streaked eastward across the sky. With any luck they'd get there before the bad guys.

Speaking of bad guys . . .

Goofball, Max, and Calamity were

already several states across the country by now. But they were flying a beat-up old crop duster, while Melvin and Candace were zipping along at superhero speed.

Calamity spotted them in his rearview mirror. "Bad news, boys," he said.

"Don't tell me," Max said. "We're going to make like a Beederman and crash."

"No, but funny you should mention him." Calamity pointed behind him. "Superheroes at six o'clock!"

Sure enough, Melvin and Candace were coming up fast.

"Do something!" Goofball screamed.

"Do what?"

"Go faster!"

"I'm going as fast as I can." It was true—he was. Melvin and Candace would be on them any second.

And then it happened. For the first time in his life, Calamity Wayne had an idea. A good idea. A whopper of an idea.

"Grab hold of something, boys. This is going to be tricky." He pulled back on the steering, and the plane veered skyward and disappeared into a cloud.

"I can't see a thing," Goofball complained.

"Perfect!" Calamity said. "Melvin and Candace won't be able to spot us."

"Am I losing my mind?" Melvin asked Candace as they sped along.

"Most likely," Candace said.

"No, I mean I thought I saw a red plane. It's gone."

"Oh. Yeah. I saw it, too."

But now there was nothing. There

was no plane at all. Except for the clouds above them, the sky was clear to the horizon. Melvin took off his glasses and cleaned them.

Suddenly a red propeller plane dropped out of the clouds. On the side was written BUBBA'S EXPERT CROP DUSTING. Before Melvin and Candace could react, the little red plane dusted them with a nasty-smelling chemical.

Melvin coughed. "Holy bug spray!"

Holy bug spray, indeed! It was almost as bad as bologna, Melvin's real weakness.

Almost.

Somewhere over east Texas, Melvin and Candace fell from the sky.

"Aaaaaaahhhhhh!"

"Great shot!" said Goofball.

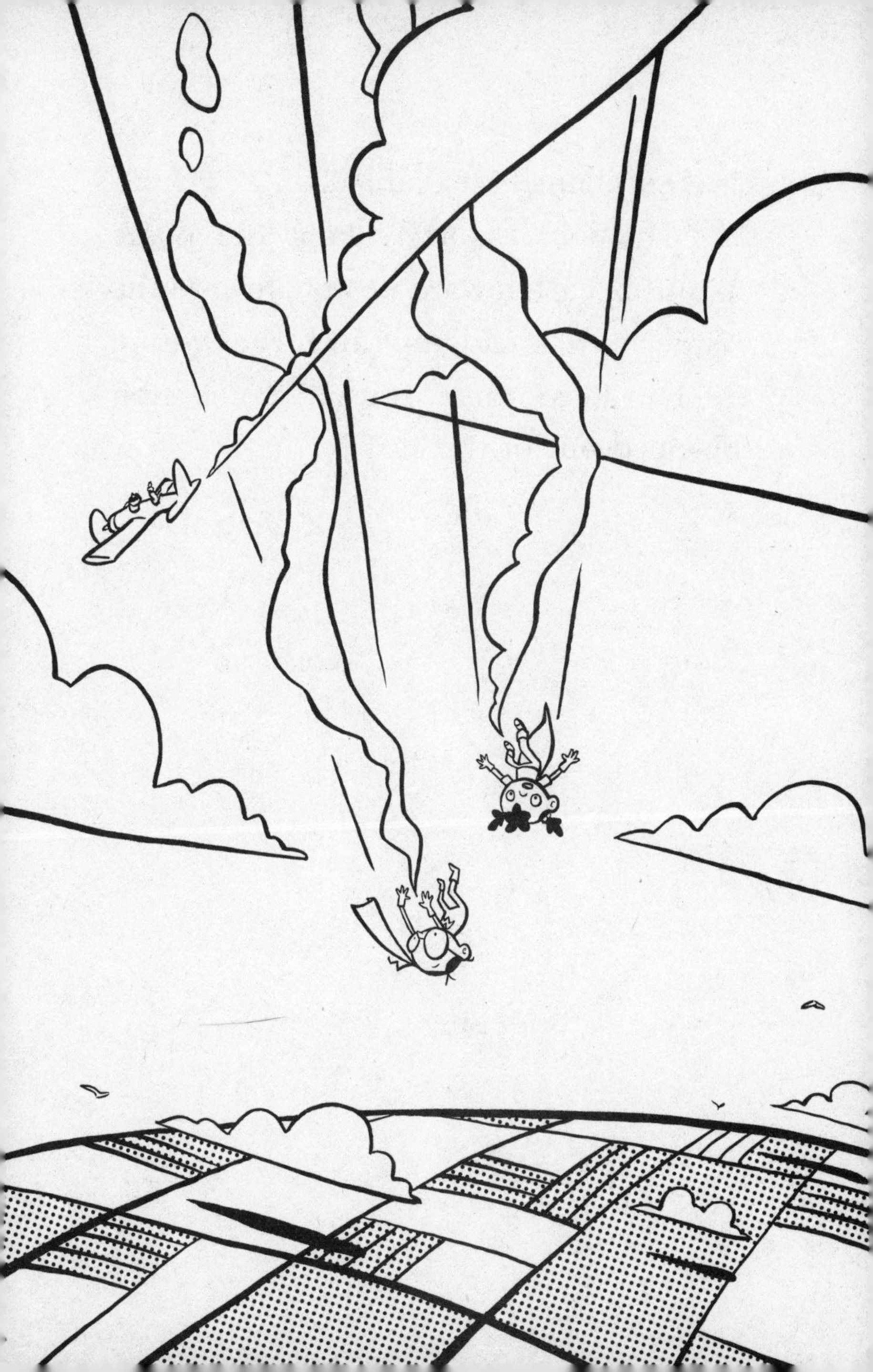

"Excellent," Max added.

"Thanks." Calamity kept the plane pointing east, toward Boston, toward the Superhero Academy and the young Melvin Beederman. Nothing could stop them now.

# TROUBLE AT NACHO'S

"Aaaaaaahhhhhh!"

It was the worst possible place for a crash landing. Not only was it east Texas. Not only were they two thousand miles away from their destination. But their fall from the sky landed them in Nacho's Amazing Reptile Show and Cactus Farm.

"Ouch," said Melvin as he finally came to a stop.

They spent the next hour removing cactus needles from each other and wrestling alligators who had mistaken them for an easy lunch. The alligators, of course, were no match for a couple of superheroes. The rattlesnakes didn't know this, and they too joined in the battle. Then the bullfrogs jumped in— and the boa constrictors.

It was the best free-for-all anyone had ever seen. The customers loved it. Nacho himself offered Melvin and Candace a job. "You'll both be rich," he said.

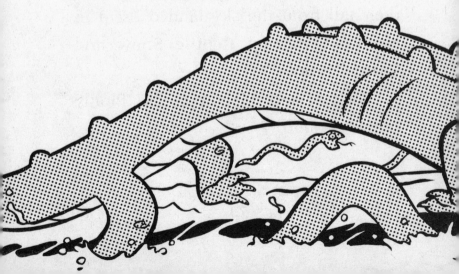

Actually, he meant that *he'd* be rich, but Melvin and Candace had other plans. They had a world to save.

More important, they had the young Melvin to save.

"Thanks, but we have to get going." Melvin looked east. "Up, up, and away!"

*Crash!*

*Splat!*

*Thud!*

*Kabonk!*

"I really loved wrestling those alligators," Candace told him as they streaked toward the horizon.

"I know," Melvin said. Candace had the best headlock he had ever seen.

"What was that move you put on that boa?" Candace asked. "It was amazing."

"I call it the pretzel. Couldn't you tell?"

Calamity brought the little red plane down in a field outside of Boston. The trio of bad guys then looked around for a car to steal to make the rest of the trip to the academy. There were no cars in the area, so they settled for a bicycle. Since Calamity was the getaway person, he pedaled, while Max and Goofball stayed on any way they could.

The academy stood up on Hero Hill overlooking Sinister Street and Devious Drive. It was almost dark when Max, Goofball, and Calamity arrived. Students of the academy were just coming in from a long day of stopping trains, rescuing damsels, and flying. At least the second-year students had been flying. The first years had not yet received their capes and were involved in simpler tasks. The young Melvin Beederman was one of the first years.

"Holy sitting duck," Goofball said, adding his evil laugh. "This is going to be easy."

Holy sitting duck, indeed! But the narrator can't say if it's going to be easy or not. That would give away the story.

They waited in the bushes outside the academy until late into the night, when the lights were out and all was quiet inside. Then they headed in to get Melvin.

"Time to make our move, boys," Goofball said.

"Don't mind if I do," Max said. "Let's make like some bad guys and kidnap a future superhero."

"Yes, let's," Calamity added.

## CALAMITY HAS
## NOGGIN POWER...ALMOST

They worked their way around the Superhero Academy, checking doors and windows.

"What if there's an alarm system?" Max asked.

Goofball shook his head. "There won't be. Who, in their right mind, would break in to a place full of super-heroes?"

"Good point," Max said. They continued around the building, but there were no unlocked doors or windows. "What do we do now?"

Goofball stepped back and looked up. He pointed to a window on the second floor. "Is that an open window, or am I seeing things?"

"Looks open, but how to get to it?" Max said.

"Drainpipe?" Calamity suggested.

Goofball and Max turned to him. Two ideas in one day? That had to be some kind of record for Calamity Wayne. There was a drainpipe running from the top of the building to the ground. It was right by the window. It might work.

"Okay, Calamity. You had the idea— you climb," Goofball said. It was so wonderful to be the boss.

Calamity Wayne's mouth dropped

open. "Me? I drive the getaway vehicle."

"And I'm the muscle," Max added.

"Well, I'm the brains," Goofball said. "And this brain says you climb. Before the sun rises would be a good idea. Now get going, Calamity."

Calamity thought he might stop coming up with ideas if this was how it was going to be. He started up the drainpipe. When he was through the window, he looked down. "Now what?"

"Go downstairs and open the door. And be quiet!"

Goofball and Max went around to the front entrance. A short time later, Calamity met them there and opened the door.

"Now to find Melvin Beederman,"

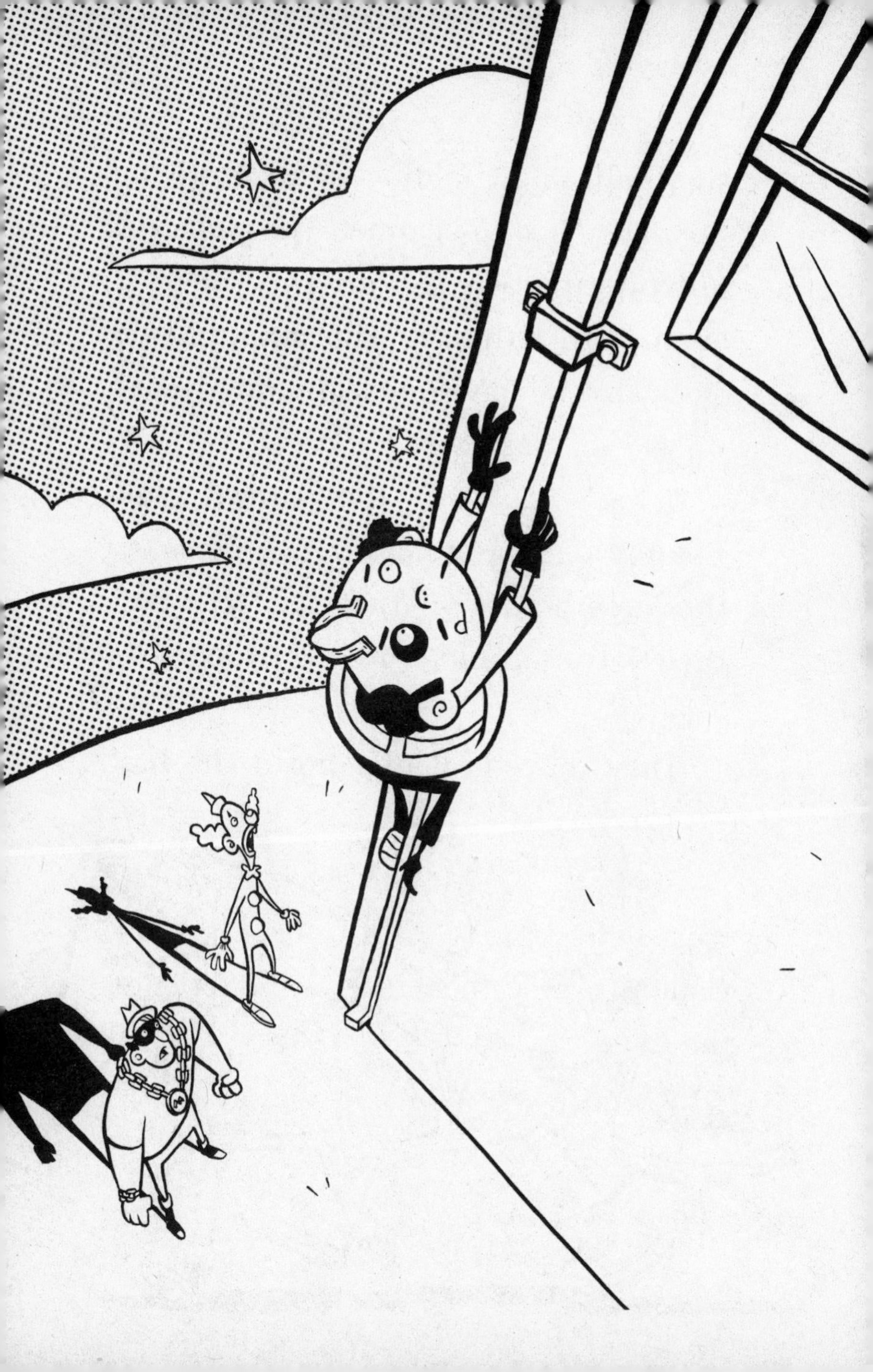

Goofball said, holding a finger to his lips. They had to be quiet. The place was full of superheroes with superhearing, among other things. "That reminds me. Does anyone have on clean underwear?"

"Never," said Max.

"That's against the rules," said Calamity. It was an old trick—gross out the superheroes so that they can't do their job. It could work . . . you never knew.

They moved silently down the hall,

checking doors. The first floor had class-rooms, teachers' offices, and a cafeteria. After making the rounds, they found a staircase and went up.

"How are we going to find him?" Max whispered.

"Look for the hair," Goofball replied. "No one else has hair like Melvin Beederman."

It was true. Melvin's hair was unique. He could be spotted a mile away. But little did they know that Melvin slept with his head beneath the covers.

While the bad guys were at the academy looking for the younger Melvin, the older version was racing along with his sidekick, getting closer and closer to Boston and the Superhero Academy.

Were they already too late? Would they get there in time to save the day? The narrator isn't saying.

Don't you hate that?

## MELVIN'S UNCLE WHO?

You may be asking yourself why, with all the extra-sensitive hearing at the academy, no one was popping up, saying "Not so fast" or some other superhero lingo. The answer is that superheroes don't sleep with their capes on. The ones at the academy didn't, anyway. No cape, no sensitive hearing. It was as simple as that.

Wait a minute. Was that simple?

The three bad guys crept down the hall of the second floor. This was indeed where the students slept. They checked every room until they found a kid with a J hairdo. This was Superhero James, of course. On the other side of the room slept Melvin Beederman.

Goofball and his companions didn't know this. They just saw a lump under the covers. Goofball pulled the blanket back, and there he was—the younger, uncaped version of Melvin Beederman.

Max grabbed him by the ankle and lifted him. He tried to cover Melvin's mouth with his other hand, but not before Melvin yelped. This woke up James, who looked like he was on the verge of yelping himself. Max quickly tossed Melvin over to Goofball and

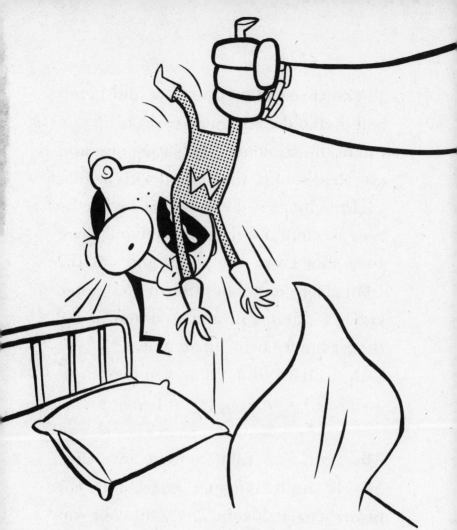

Calamity, who gagged him, then he went
after James.

But James was no match for the

thick-necked Max. One swat and James was out cold.

"Let's go before anyone wakes up," Goofball said.

They hurried down the hall with the now bound-and-gagged Melvin. Then they shot down the stairs and out the front door. You should have seen three bad guys and a future superhero make their getaway on a single bike.

In fact, Mr. Illustrator, you're on!

The sun was just coming up when Melvin and Candace arrived at the Superhero Academy. The front door was wide open. "Not a good sign," Melvin said.

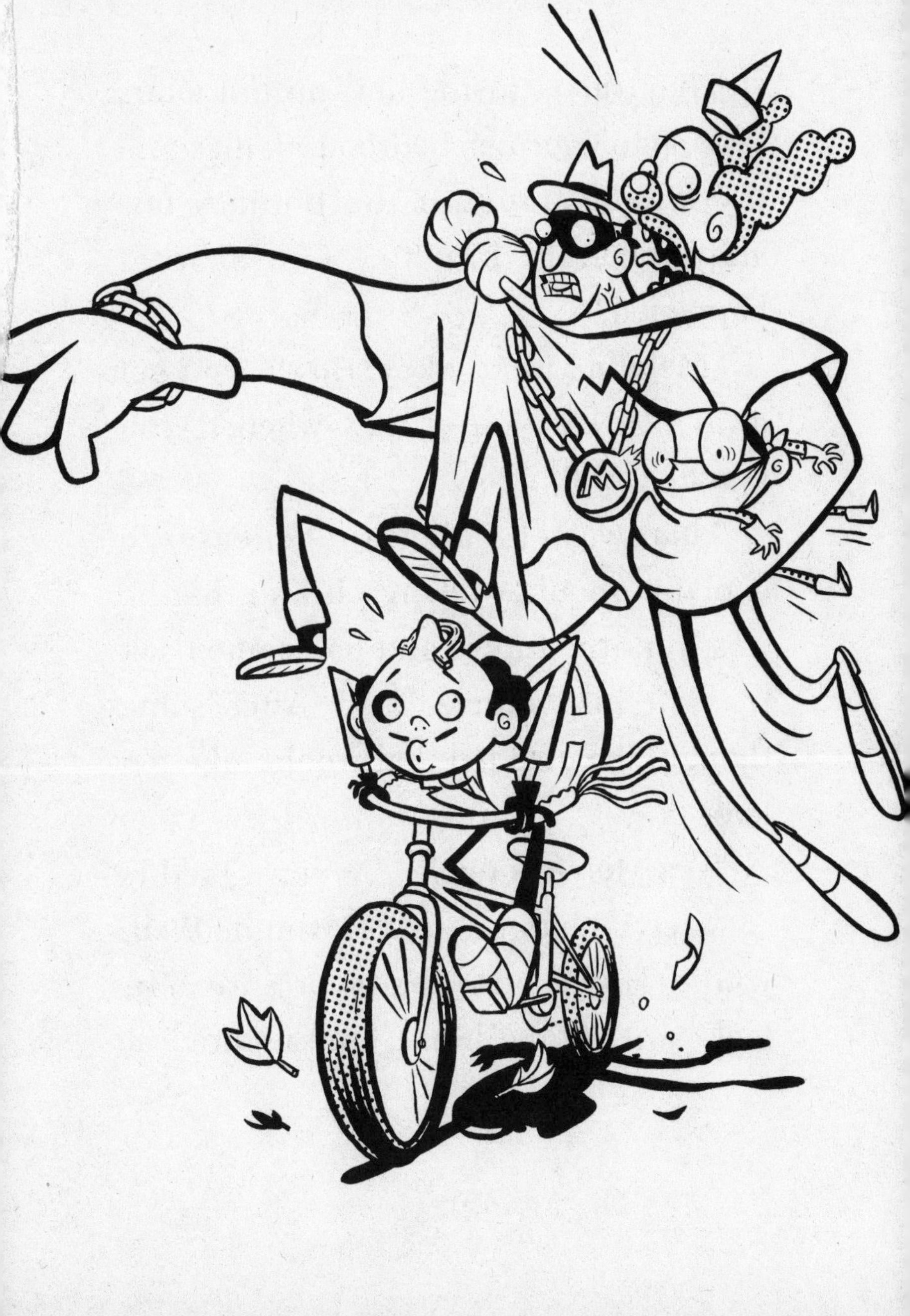
M

They raced inside and up the stairs to Melvin's former bedroom. James still lay unconscious on the floor. A few slaps brought him to. "James, what happened?"

"Melvin, you're okay. How'd you get away? How'd you— Hey, where'd you get the cape?"

This wasn't going to be easy to explain. Should Melvin tell him that he was from the future and had come back to save his younger self? After some thought, he decided that would take too long.

"I'm Melvin's uncle . . . uh . . . Fred."

"Melvin has an uncle? Hmm. Well, you look like him, that's for sure. You look *exactly* like him." James stared at

Melvin. Everything about him was the same. The hair. The freckles. The buckteeth.

"Yep, that's me. Uncle Fred. Where's Melvin?"

"There were three of them," James said. "One of them had an enormous neck and an even bigger fist." He touched his head lightly where it still hurt. "One punch is all it took."

Melvin and Candace exchanged looks. "Max the Wonder Thug," they said together. They'd know that oversized neck and fist anywhere.

"Which way did they go?" Melvin asked.

James shook his head. "Beats me. I was unconscious, remember?"

"Do you have a Lair Hill in town, by any chance?" Candace asked.

"No, but we have a Sinister Street, which is right next to Devious Drive," James said. "Will that work?"

"Lead the way," Melvin said.

James, Melvin, and Candace left the building. The question was: Were they already too late?

## MELVIN HAS LEFT THE BUILDING

Of course, you already know that Melvin has left the building. It's how the last chapter ended, but the narrator just wanted to name this chapter that for some reason. It's a narrator thing.

"Up, up, and away."

Once outside the two superheroes launched themselves. At least Candace did. While she was waiting for Melvin to join her in the air, she didn't do her nails or juggle tangerines. This was because she was carrying James, who didn't have his cape yet and couldn't fly.

*Crash!*

*Splat!*

*Thud!*

*Kabonk!*

James had never seen a superhero have so much trouble getting up in the air. The Melvin he knew had not yet received his cape. James looked at Candace for some kind of explanation.

"Don't ask," she said.

And so James didn't. He pointed out the way to Sinister Street and Devious Drive. "It's over there, next to Ruffian Road and Bad Guy Boulevard."

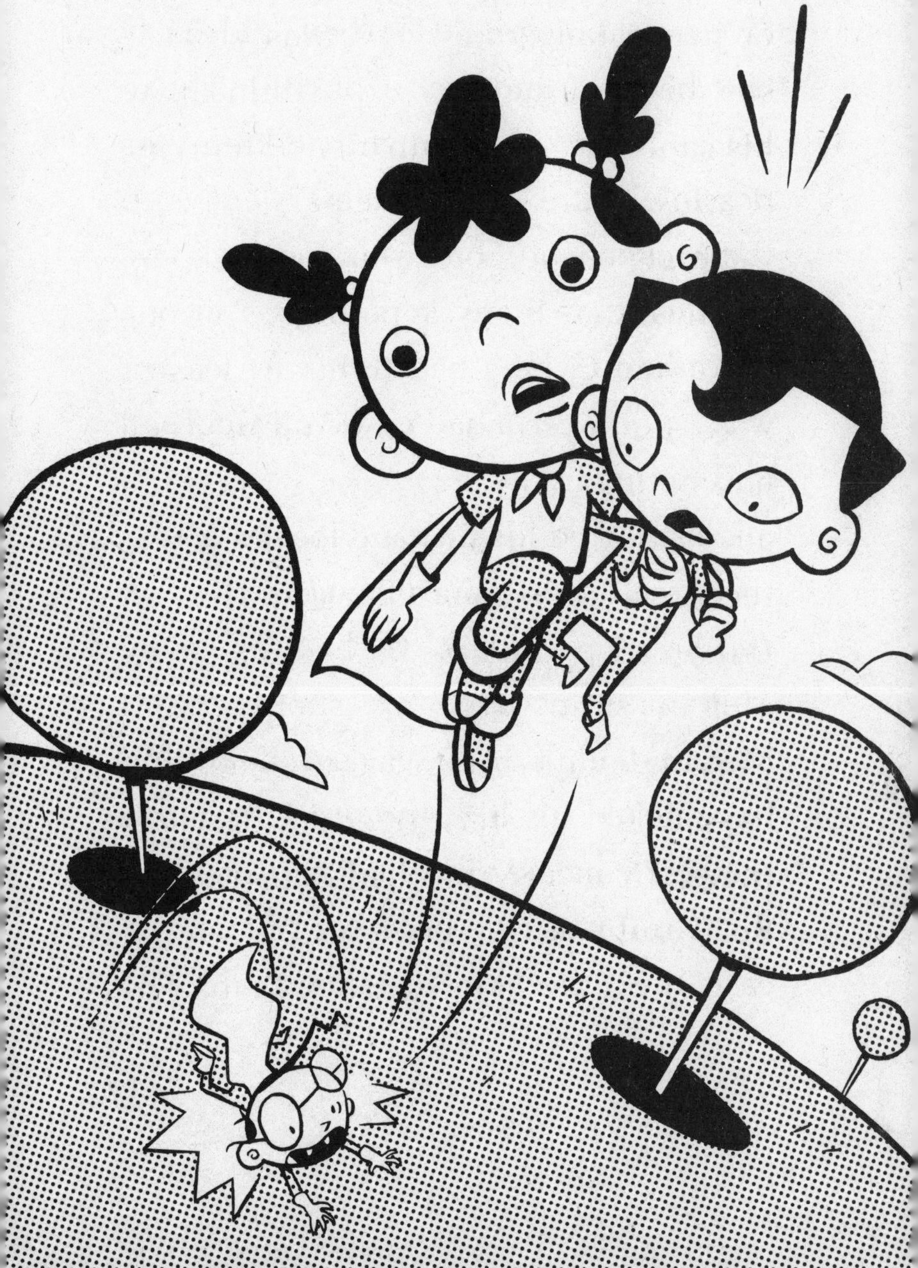

"We need bologna," Goofball said. They had been running most of the night to get as far away from the academy as possible. Sure, the students slept with their capes off, but you never knew. Besides, that many superheroes in one place had to be a bad thing. At least it was if you were a bad guy. And Goofball and Company were.

Max licked his lips and looked across the street at Priscilla's Pancake Heaven. "I'd prefer pancakes." He had the young Melvin slung over his shoulders. If Melvin hadn't been gagged he would have licked his lips, too. Priscilla made the best pancakes on the East Coast.

"Not for us. We need the bologna in case the other Melvin shows up. The superhero version, I mean. Bologna is his weakness."

Calamity shook his head. "Melvin is history. I dusted him and his little side-kick with bug spray. They fell on a pair of cactus and got eaten by alligators."

"Yeah," Goofball said, "but what about the narrator? It would be like him to bring Melvin back. And you watch, it will be just in the nick of time or something."

It was too distressing to argue about. It was as though the narrator wanted the main character to win. Bologna was what they needed, Goofball decided. Just in case the other Melvin Beederman came back—not to mention Candace Brinkwater.

They found an open butcher shop on East Ruffian. Goofball went inside, banged his fist on the counter, and said, "Bologna! And give it to me on dirty paper!"

# MARGARET TAKES THE CAPE

Now, armed with a good supply of
bologna, Goofball, Max, and Calamity
set about doing away with the young
Melvin Beederman. But how to do it?
That was the question. And where?
Sometimes the *where* was as important
as the *how*. They already knew the *who*
and the *why*. And the *what* was in there
someplace. Sometimes *what* got lost in
the shuffle. *How* and *where* got most of

the attention, which could be very annoying if you were a *what*.

Wow, this is getting confusing. But back to our story.

"We need to get out of sight," Goofball said. "The sun is coming up. There can't be any witnesses." This was part of the Bad Guy's Code: Do your sinister and devious deeds in secret so you don't get caught.

The trio was down by the waterfront, and the sky was getting lighter by the minute. Max pointed to what looked like an abandoned building on a pier over the water.

"Perfect," Goofball said. Unfortunately, the place was locked. But they did not call Max the muscle for nothing. "Max, break it down."

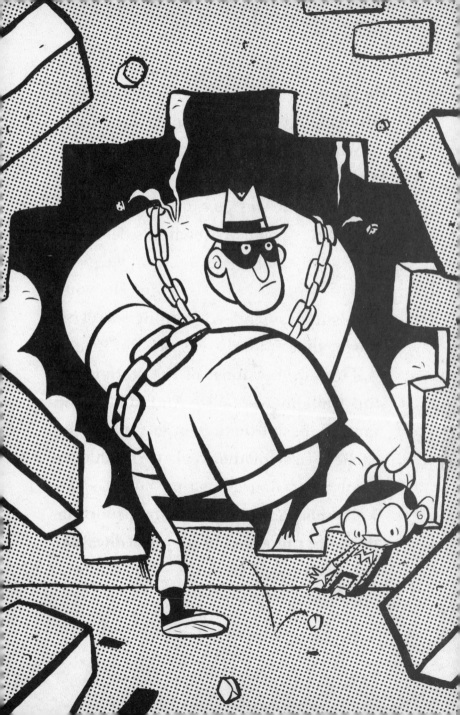

Max had broken down many doors in his life, but making a doorway where none existed sounded like even more fun. And so with his mighty fist, he did. One punch and it was complete. He dragged the young, uncaped Melvin inside.

The sun was indeed coming up. This meant that not only was most of Boston waking up, but most of the students at the academy were also. And Melvin and James's best friend, Margaret, was the earliest riser of them all. It didn't take her long to figure out that her two pals were missing. She came to their room every morning so that they could walk to breakfast together.

But today they were not there. She checked the lump of blankets on Melvin's bed. Nothing. She ran down the hall to see if they'd gone on ahead of her. They hadn't. They were simply missing.

"Holy mystery!" she said to herself. "I smell a rat."

Holy mystery, indeed! Actually she didn't smell anything. She was a first-year student and hadn't received her cape yet. Without a cape, she didn't have an extra-sensitive nose. She didn't have extra-sensitive hearing. And, of course, she couldn't fly. They received flight instruction starting in the first year, but it was all done in flight simulators. Still, Margaret knew something was wrong; her two friends were in trouble. She could feel it—even if she couldn't quite smell it.

She knew she needed all the powers of a superhero to find her friends. She needed a cape. Wasn't there a second-year student who owed her a favor? Hadn't she and Melvin helped someone with math? She stood in the hallway and thought about this.

Nope. She hadn't helped anyone. No one owed her a favor. She'd have to steal a cape to find Melvin and James, which had to be against the Superhero's Code. But Melvin and James were in trouble and sometimes you just had to break the rules, didn't you? Just ask the narrator about that. And so she ran to the boys' shower room, covered her eyes, and

poked around for the first thing that felt like a cape, grabbed it, and ran out again.

"Up, up, and away!" She was a natural. She flew down the hall and out an open window.

"Melvin and James, where are you?" she called. Then she cupped an ear and listened with her extra-sensitive hearing for their response.

# THE HOLE-IN-THE-WALL GANG

"That's Margaret!" the caped Melvin said.

"What?" James said.

"Margaret is calling for us . . . uh . . . I mean, you and Melvin. At least she sounds like someone who might be named Margaret."

"Wow, you have great hearing."

"It's the cape. Standard academy issue," Melvin said. "I graduated in the year two blah blah blah."

"Blah blah blah?"

"Yes, it's a secret. I don't want to date this book. So who's Margaret?"

"She's Melvin's and my best friend. She must have realized we're missing."

Melvin nodded. "That can't be helped now. There was no time to leave a note for her."

They were flying over East Ruffian. Candace pointed to a butcher shop. "Stay clear of that place," she said. "Where there's meat, there's bologna."

They did. They'd already been knocked out of the sky by bug spray; they didn't need to be done in by lunch meat. It had happened before, and it wasn't enjoyable in the least.

They searched and searched. First down Bad Guy Boulevard. Then up

Devious Drive. They even poked around Wicked Way.

"Better try the waterfront," James said. "Lots of abandoned warehouses down there. It's evil lair city, if you know what I mean."

Candace did. So did Melvin.

While Melvin, Candace, and James were busy looking for the bad guys, Goofball and Company were getting ready to dispose of the younger Melvin—the uncaped version. They looked around the abandoned building on the pier. It wasn't a warehouse. It was just an unoccupied building full of dusty medicine balls and rusty barbells. It was the former location of Fast Freddy's Fitness Center and Fishing Supplies.

"Barbells," Goofball said. "I have an idea, boys." He turned to Max. "Make a hole in the floor, Max."

Max punched the floor. "Done."

Goofball looked through the newly created hole at the water below. "Now, tie Melvin to one of the barbells, the heaviest one."

"Using what?" Max scanned the floor.

"Ungag him and use that," Goofball said.

They ungagged Melvin and that's when he screamed. "Help! Margaret! James! Help!"

"Help!"

Margaret knew the sound of Melvin's voice when she heard it. She was just passing over a butcher shop on East Ruffian and veered toward the waterfront, where the sound seemed to be coming from.

But she was not the only one who heard it.

"That's me screaming!" the caped Melvin said. "Uh . . . I mean, that's Melvin." He and Candace, who was still holding James, sped toward the sound of the screaming. If only they could get there in the nick of time!

# THE HOLE-IN-THE-*FLOOR* GANG?

"Shut him up," Goofball said as Calamity and Max tied Melvin to the barbell.

Max made a fist, and that's all it took for Melvin to stop screaming. He'd seen the thug use that fist on James. He did not want the same to happen to him.

"Okay, he's tied," Calamity said. "Now what?"

"Drop him through that hole and our superhero problems will be over."

"You mean we can make like a tree and leave?" Max asked.

"We can make like bad guys and start robbing banks again." Goofball pointed to the hole in the floor. "Toss him in and let's get out of—"

"Not so fast!" Melvin, Candace, and James appeared suddenly. It was Melvin's turn to kick in the door, but when they saw the hole in the wall created by Max's fist, they went through that instead.

Melvin moved forward. "Untie me . . . uh . . . I mean, untie the boy."

Goofball smiled. "Are you forgetting something?" He tossed a huge slab of bologna that landed at Melvin's feet.

Melvin instantly felt weak. The room began to spin. Then he fell to his knees.

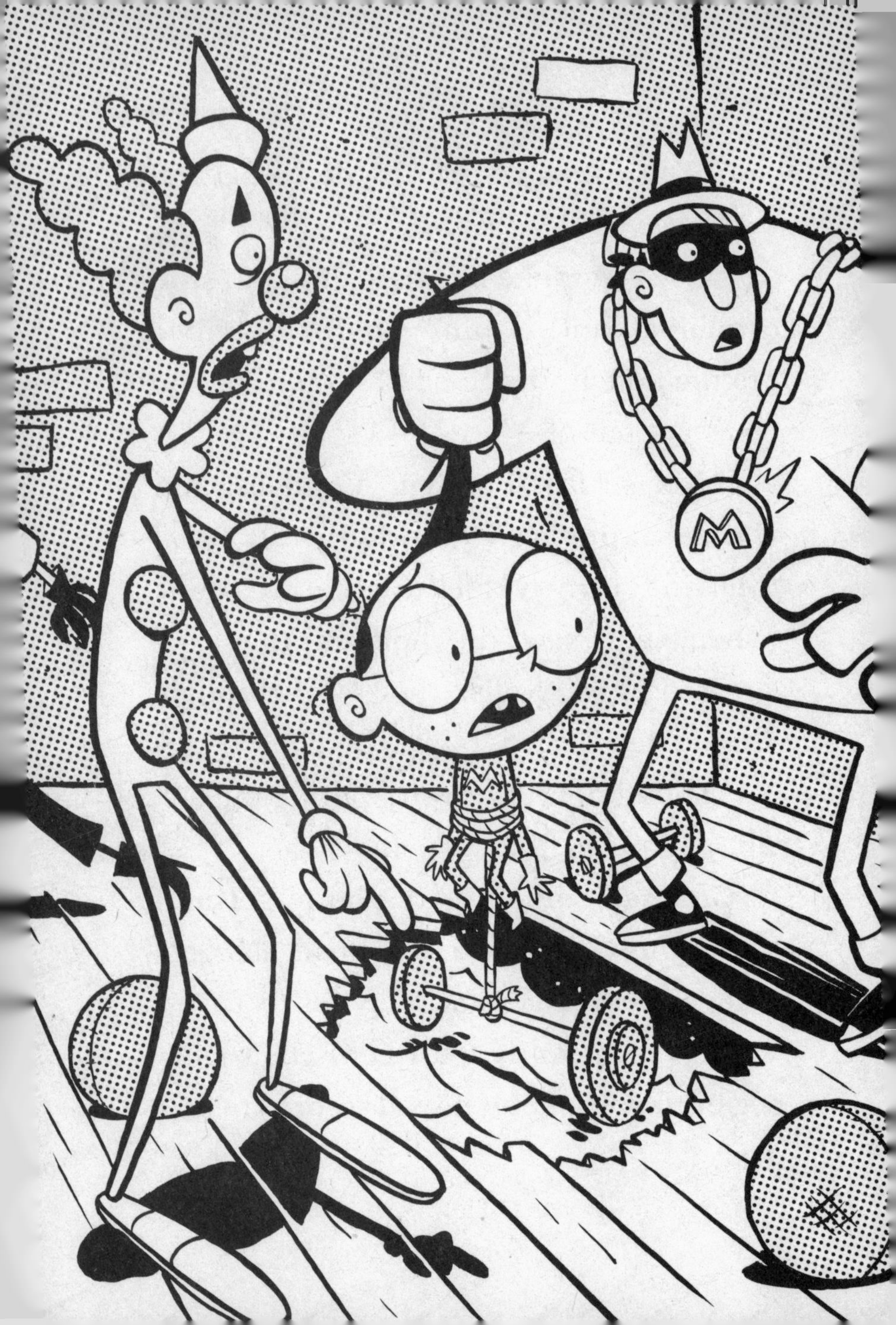

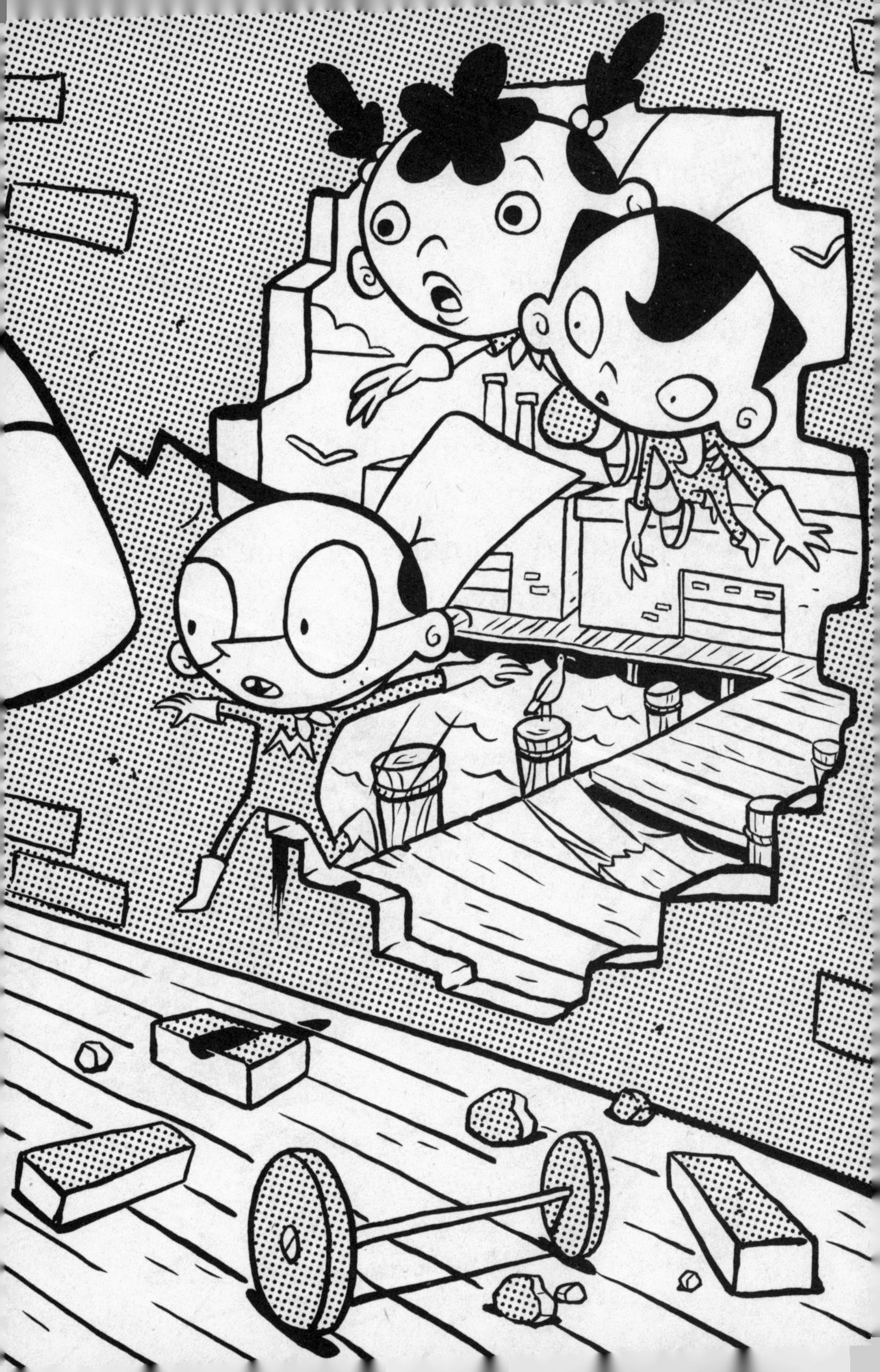

"Can't . . . move . . . get . . . me . . . out . . . of . . . here," he gasped.

A second later Candace was on the ground beside him. "Can't . . . move . . . get . . . me . . . out . . . of . . . here."

James, who had no cape, and therefore had no weaknesses, looked confused. "What's with the 'can't move' stuff?"

Goofball put his head back and laughed—his evil laugh, his award-winning evil laugh. He turned to his friends. "Max, Calamity, tie them all up. Tie them all to the barbell and drop them in the hole. Use your shoelaces if you have to."

Max and Calamity rushed across the room and grabbed Melvin, Candace, and James. This was not difficult, since Superhero Melvin and Superhero Candace had lost their strength, and James was just a boy with no superpowers at all.

"Tie them up," Goofball said again.

*Crash!* The door to the building tore from its hinges and landed in a cloud of dust on the floor. In popped the caped

Margaret. "Not so fast!" Then she looked at the door she'd just kicked down and said, "I *loved* doing that!"

She moved forward and scanned the faces in the room—Goofball McCluskey, Max the Wonder Thug, Calamity Wayne.

Suddenly she felt weak. She fell to her knees gasping, "Can't . . . move . . . get . . . me . . . out . . . of . . . here." Her cape was different from the one worn by Melvin and Candace, so bologna wasn't her weakness. But guys named Wayne were.

Goofball didn't know any of this. He just saw another superhero who was obviously, and thankfully, powerless. The bad guy business was getting better and better. "Tie her up, too."

# MELVIN HAS TWO SIDEKICKS

While the arrival of Margaret distracted the bad guys, Candace was busy slipping her nail file to the younger, uncaped Melvin Beederman. She had just enough strength left to do this. And the younger Melvin was not affected by the bologna.

"Use it to cut us loose," Candace whispered.

The two Melvins, Candace, James, and Margaret, along with sacks of bologna, were now strapped to an enormous barbell. Max, the muscle, dropped it all through the hole in the floor and down they went—*Splash!*—into the water.

Goofball, Max, and Calamity stood at the edge of the hole, watching. "If I was not in such a hurry to get back home, I would stand here and have a nice long evil laugh session," Goofball said. He paused. "Oh, what the heck. *Mwaah haa haa haa!*"

See? You *can* tell why the guy is an award winner.

"That felt good. Let's find that plane and get out of here."

"Make like a crop duster and leave them in our dust?" Max said. He was running out of things to "make like," and

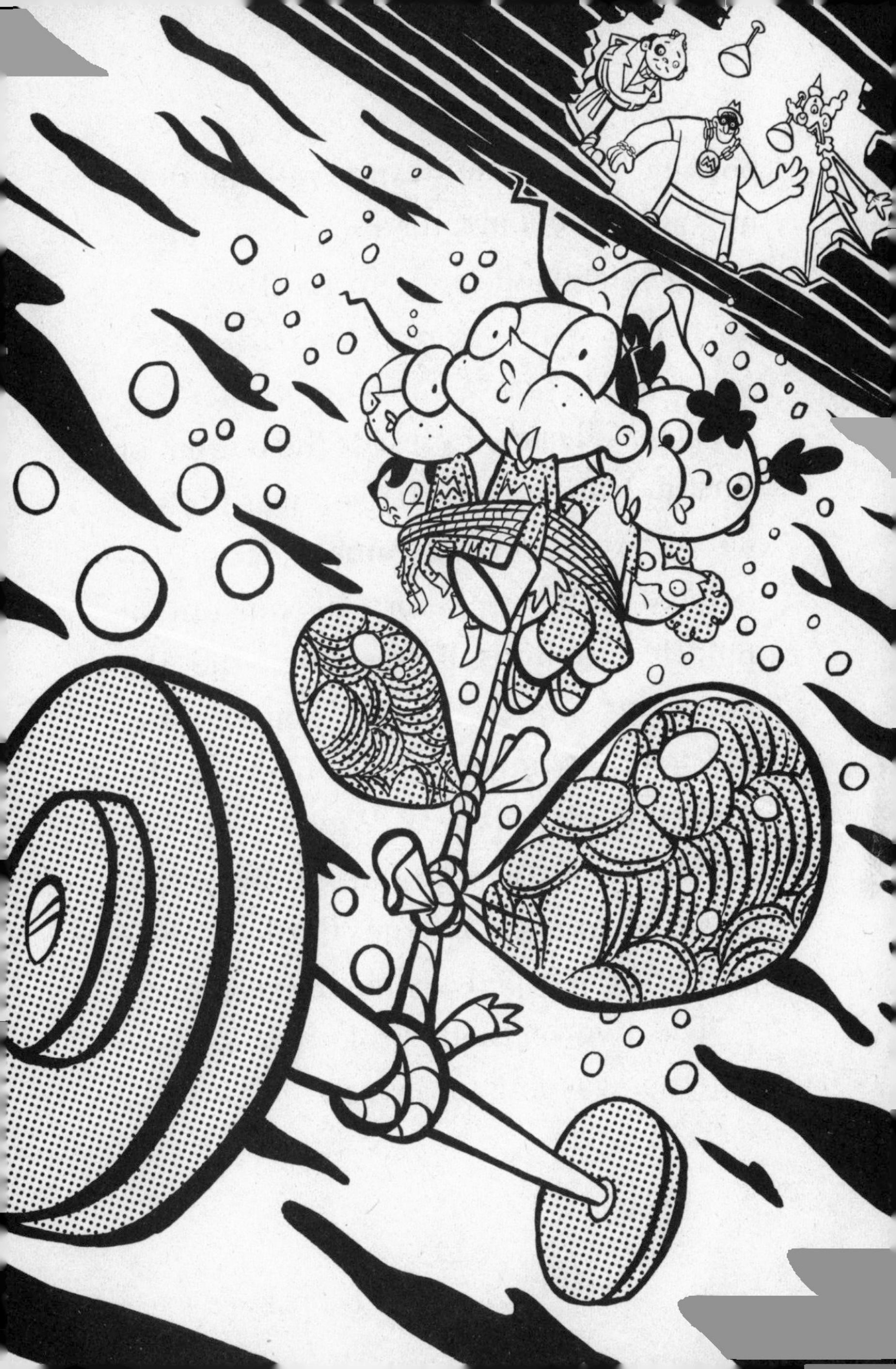

it was getting on everyone's nerves. Including the narrator's!

"Whatever."

The barbell came to rest at the bottom of Boston Harbor, and the younger Melvin got to work cutting himself loose. He worked quickly—before he ran out of air. He cut himself free, then did the same for James. At the same time, Margaret, who was no longer in the presence of Calamity Wayne, felt her strength return. She busted the shoelaces tying her to the barbell, then grabbed the caped Melvin and Candace.

The five of them broke the surface together, gasping for breath.

"Holy suffocation!" Melvin said. "That was a close one."

Holy suffocation, indeed! It sure was. They climbed back into the abandoned building.

The young Melvin looked at the slightly older, caped version of himself. "That's a great head of hair you've got. Are we related?"

"Uh . . . I'm your uncle Fred," said the older Melvin. He didn't know how to tell him the truth. And besides, he had bad guys to catch.

"Uncle Fred? How come I've never heard of you?"

"No time to explain." The caped Melvin then turned to Candace and Margaret. "Three bad guys and three superheroes. Perfect. I can go after Goofball. Candace, you can get Max. Margaret, you've got Calamity."

They ran outside and launched themselves. "Up, up, and away!" Candace and Margaret were up and flying on the first try. Melvin did things his way—*Crash! Splat! Thud! Kabonk!* It wasn't pretty, but then again, it never was.

"What's the plan, boss?" Calamity asked. He knew they had to make like a something and do something, but he wasn't sure what either something was.

"We split up, just in case," Goofball replied.

"Just in case what?"

"Just in case something happens. You know, Melvin and his noggin power, or maybe the narrator will pull a fast one. You never know."

Yes, you sure don't.

And so Goofball headed north, Max south, and Calamity west.

"Not so fast!" Melvin said, dropping out of the sky and landing right in front of Goofball.

"Curses!" Goofball muttered, which is a very common bad guy expression, especially at the end of a book.

Goofball did not even try to get away. Melvin had him, and both of them knew it.

"Stop trying to get away from me!" Candace said as she plopped herself down in front of Max on the other side of town.

"Don't you mean 'not so fast'?" Max asked. It was, after all, part of the Superhero's Code to say that. But Candace hadn't graduated from the academy and didn't know the correct lingo.

But no matter, Max was caught, just like Goofball. The problem was, where was Margaret?

At that moment she was dropping out of the sky and planting herself on the sidewalk in front of Calamity Wayne. "Not so fast!" she said. She was a student at the academy; she knew the code.

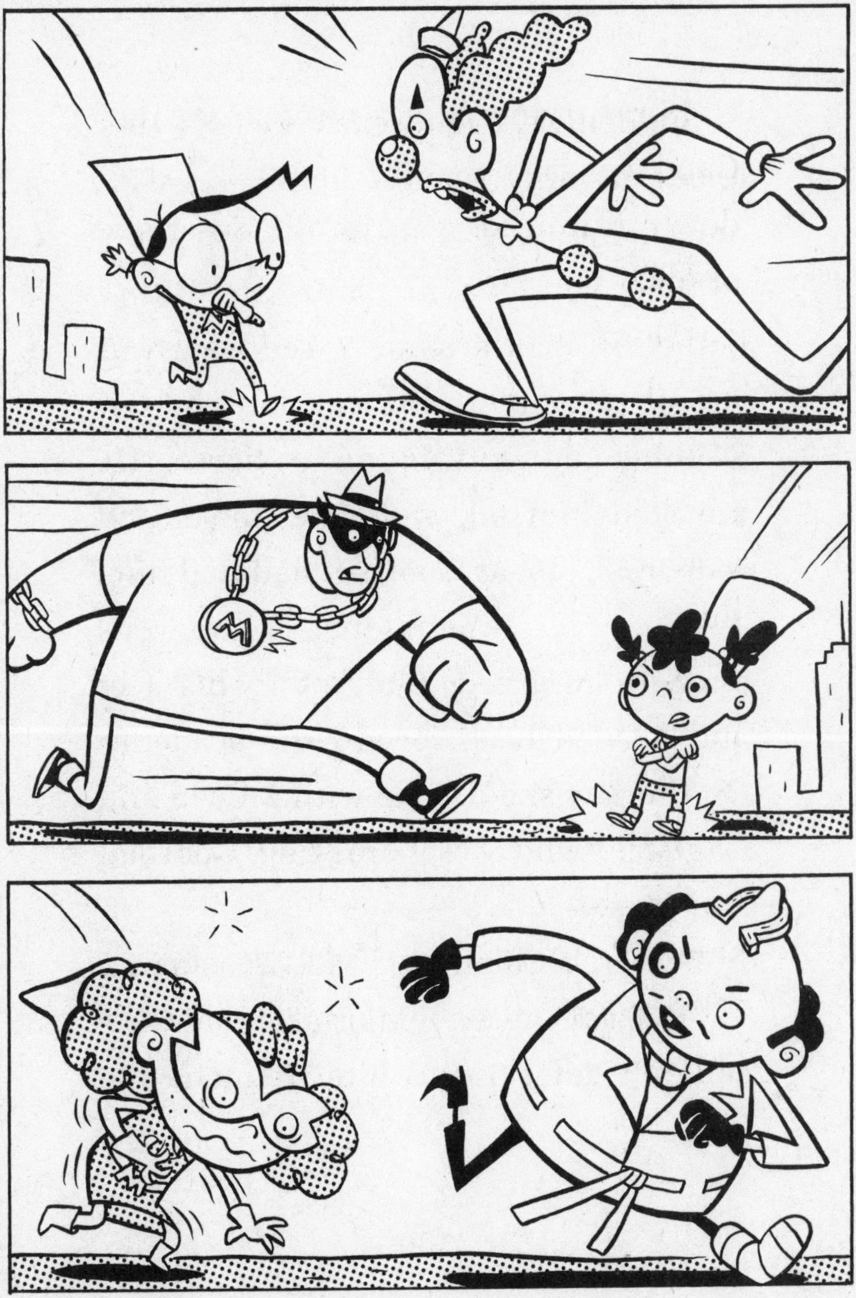

Suddenly she felt weak. She fell to her knees, gasping, "Can't . . . move . . . get . . . me . . . out . . . of . . . here."

"See ya," Wayne said. He didn't bother to stick around to see what was wrong. He ran. A short time later he saw a policeman sitting on a horse. He knocked him off, stole the horse, and rode west, just as Goofball had told him.

After he was gone, Margaret's strength returned. She got to her feet and headed back toward the academy. On the way she met up with Melvin and Candace, who were dragging Goofball and Max.

"Where's Calamity?" Melvin asked.

"He got away," Margaret said. "I couldn't get close to him. It made me weak."

"Weak in the knees?"

"Yes."

"Hmm." Melvin stroked his chin. "Sounds like a crush. Sounds like you have the hots for Calamity Wayne."

"Sounds like it's the cape," Candace said. She turned to Melvin. "Should we go after him?"

Melvin shook his head. "We've got the brains of the operation and we've also got the muscle. Who cares about the get-away guy?"

And so Melvin and Candace flew back to Los Angeles along with Goofball and Max. Then they used the time machine to return to the proper time. *Clankity–Whump–Pow–Thunk!* It was the worst re-entry yet. But it didn't bother Melvin or Candace one bit. They were

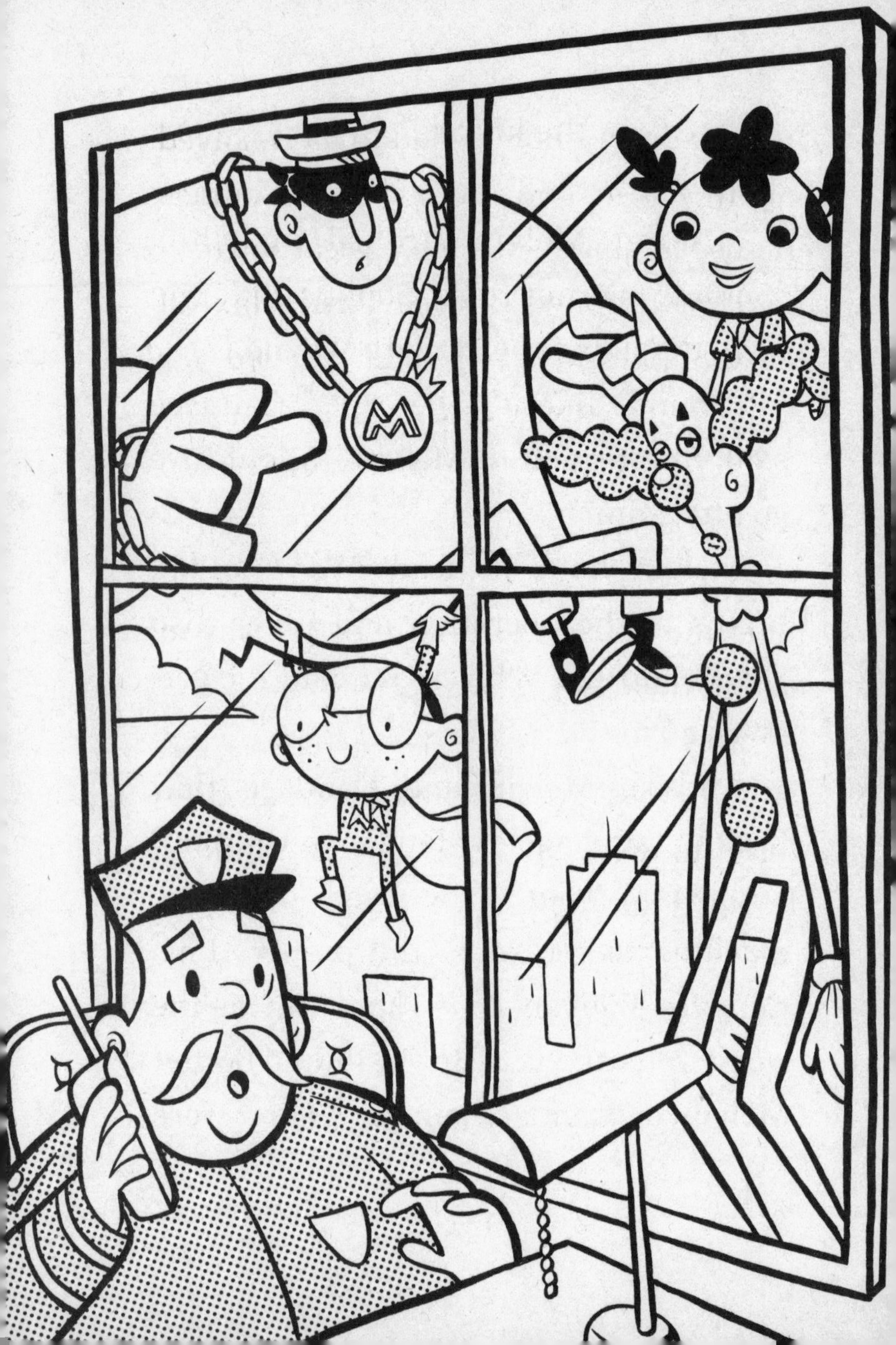

just glad to be home, glad to have solved another case, and very glad to be super-heroes in charge of such a great town.

They dropped Goofball and Max off at the police station and headed for home.

"Save the world again tomorrow?" Melvin asked.

"Of course," said his partner in uncrime. "I can't think of a better way to spend the day."

And so they did, because it was what superheroes do, and it was what they *loved* to do . . . just as soon as Candace finished her math.

*And now, a superheroic excerpt from*

## MELVIN BEEDERMAN SUPERHERO

BOOK 8

## INVASION FROM PLANET DORK

"Holy this-is-an-emergency!"

Superhero Melvin Beederman had been enjoying a long shower while singing one of his favorite Grateful Fred songs—"Love Is a Nose but You Better Not Pick It." All was well in his world. He toweled off, rubbed some Melvin Mousse into his hair, forming a perfect *M*, flexed in front of the mirror, and went to see about breakfast. Was there a pretzel in the house? There was not. That's what you call an emergency.

Holy this-is-an-emergency, indeed! It sure was. Even Melvin's pet rat Hugo had something to say on the subject.

"Squeak," he said with a twitch of his whiskers. This either meant "Get me some pretzels, and make it snappy," or "You were a little flat on 'Love Is a Nose but You Better Not Pick It.'" Melvin was never exactly sure what Hugo was saying. He just knew he wanted pretzels as much as his rat did. Maybe more.

Melvin and Hugo lived together in a tree house overlooking the city of Los Angeles, where Melvin saved the world on a daily basis, with the help of his partner in crime, Candace Brinkwater. But this morning, work would have to wait. He needed to stock up on snacks so that he and his pet could start the day off properly, by eating pretzels, drinking root beer, and watching their favorite TV show—*The Adventures of Thunderman.*

"I'll be back in a flash," Melvin said to Hugo,

as he launched himself out the window. "Up, up, and away!"

*Crash!*

He hit the ground hard. He got to his feet and tried again.

"Up, up, and away!"

*Splat!*

He hit the ground even harder.

Once more.

"Up, up, and away!"

*Thud!*

And again.

"Up, up, and away!"

*Kabonk!*

On the fifth try he was up and flying. This was how it went with Melvin Beederman. It always took him at least five tries to get up and flying. But no matter. He was up in the air now and on a mission, which is the same thing as being on a pretzel run, but mission sounds better, so we'll go with that. As he streaked across the sky, Melvin looked down, and what did he see? Underwear—and lots of it. He couldn't turn off his x-ray vision, so he saw everyone's underwear whether he wanted to or not.

But underwear was the least of his problems. Something didn't feel right. Melvin could sense when trouble was brewing, and right now it was—or at least it was about to be. He didn't care if trouble was brewing or if it was just *thinking* about brewing. Trouble was trouble, and it was his job to do something about it.